# A BABY TO LOVE

## AMISH SECRET BABY

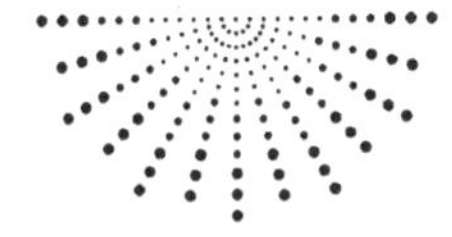

## SARAH MILLER

WWW.SWEETBOOKHUB.COM

One thing my readers have been asking for is a mini-series of interlinked books. I went back through all my memories and came up with the idea of these three stories all linked with a secret baby.

What could be better as the summer sets in than to sit and read about the amazing Amish and a wonderful baby miracle?

Enjoy these books,

Sarah

For occasional FREE books and to hear about my latest releases join my newsletter here

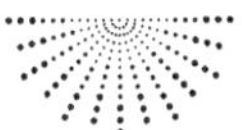

# CHAPTER ONE

FAITH'S CREEK, PENNSYLVANIA

*A* wedding was always a happy occasion in Faith's Creek, and the wedding of Leah Fisher to Adam Garrett had been particularly joyous. The whole community had turned out to celebrate. Miriam Graber could not be happier to see her friend married to the man she loved, a love they had fought so hard to realize. Miriam had been tasked with taking care of Elizabeth – the *kinner* that Leah and Adam had returned from Philadelphia with, and who they now raised as their own.

The *boppli* had been restless during the ceremony, and Miriam had taken her out three times into the fresh air, where her cries echoed across the farmyard next to the barn where the wedding was taking place. But Miriam did not mind, she loved *kinner* – *bopplis* in particular. As she was quieting Elizabeth for the third time, her friend Alma Hochstetler King emerged, holding her own *boppli*, whose name was Samuel.

"I can't keep her quiet, she's got quite a pair of lungs on her," Miriam said, bouncing Elizabeth in her arms.

"Don't worry about it. Everyone knows *bopplis* cry at weddings – they cry whenever they get a chance, usually at the worst possible time." Alma laughed. "I knew Samuel was about to start. It seems neither of them are that worried about seeing Leah and Adam married." Alma laughed again, smiling at Miriam.

The two had been friends for many years, and, along with Leah, they formed a bond of friendship more akin to sisters – though their looks were quite different, it didn't matter, with their kapps and prayer coverings in place those differences were nothing. What mattered was what was in their hearts and there, they were the same. Miriam had red hair and blue eyes, Alma had dark hair and blue eyes, and Leah had long blonde hair and brown eyes. In the Englischer world, they would be as unlike as could be imagined. But looks did not matter, only what was in their hearts. They had been through much together, and with Leah now married, it seemed another chapter in their lives was drawing to an end.

Miriam was soon to set off on her rumspringa, something she had looked forward to ever since Leah had departed for Philadelphia on hers. Alma had followed a little later, and this had only served to raise Miriam's hopes for her own experience of life beyond Faith's Creek.

"I'm so happy for them both. They've been through a lot," Miriam said.

Alma nodded. "They certainly have, we all have," she replied, kissing Samuel on the forehead.

Life had not been straightforward for either Alma or Leah. Alma had found herself the adopted *mamm* of another woman's *boppli*, a woman she had cared deeply for, and Leah and Adam had been forced to flee Philadelphia for the sake of Elizabeth's safety – her biological grandparents were unfit for the duties that were theirs. Luckily, all had ended well, and the two families were now so happy.

"I just want a nice quiet rumspringa. I'll come back, I know I will," Miriam said.

Alma laughed. "It wasn't that long ago that you were talking about never coming back," she replied.

Miriam blushed. She had always looked forward to her rumspringa. Miriam's parents could be strict, and the thought of leaving Faith's Creek and setting off for an adventure in Philadelphia had always fascinated her. But seeing her two friends settled and happy in their marriages, raising their families, and finding their place in the world, had made Miriam question her own hopes for the future. Having learned something of the outside world, she had grown somewhat nervous of what her rumspringa might reveal, and though she looked forward to it, she did so with some trepidation.

"I'll come back," she said, as Elizabeth stopped crying, her face breaking into a smile as she gurgled.

"With a *boppli*?" Alma replied, and she laughed.

Miriam shook her head and smiled. As much as she loved *kinner* – doting on Elizabeth and Samuel – she knew she was not yet ready for her own. She had seen the way the arrival of the two *bopplis* had changed the lives of her two friends forever. Miriam was determined that her own experience would be more conventional. She dreamed of getting married and settling down, of making a home, and when the time was right, of having a *boppli* of her very own. But that time was not now.

"You won't find me bringing home any stray *kinner*," she said, just as the barn doors opened and the happy couple emerged into the sunshine.

"Oh, don't they look amazing," Alma exclaimed, as Leah came hurrying over to them, holding out her arms to take Elizabeth from Miriam.

She looked ever so pretty that day, dressed in a simple outfit made by her *mamm* for the occasion, her face glowing radiantly with happiness, her long blonde hair tucked up neatly and covered over with her kapp.

"There's my beautiful little girl. Oh, come to your *mamm*," she said, taking Elizabeth from Miriam's arms.

"I brought her out because she was crying. I didn't want her disturbing everyone," Miriam said.

Leah only laughed and shook her head. "*Denke.* You did the right thing, but I wouldn't have minded. She's part of the family. We're all a family now," she said, as Adam came to join them.

"*Denke* for watching her, Miriam. I knew she'd cry," he said, kissing Elizabeth on the forehead.

"They both like a good cry every now and then," Alma said, bouncing Samuel in her arms.

"That's what *bopplis* do. Come on, now, let's celebrate. We've got a veritable feast in the barn," Leah said, and taking Elizabeth with her, she hurried off to greet the other guests, followed by Adam.

"They look so happy together, they really do," Alma said, smiling, as they watched Leah and Adam together.

"I hope my wedding day turns out as wonderful as this," Miriam said, reaching out her finger for Samuel to play with.

"You need to find a man to marry, first," Alma replied.

Miriam smiled. "I'm... working on it," she said, feeling the blush rise in her cheeks.

Miriam had had admirers, though at sixteen she was still young enough for marriage to seem a long way off, a distant possibility, though one she looked forward to. One man, in particular, had taken a shine to her. His name was Jonathan Kemp, a handsome boy of eighteen, with brown hair and deep blue eyes, he was tall and well-built. He was kind, and would often bring her small gifts, and tokens of his affection – a bar of chocolate, or a piece of wood he had carved. Miriam liked him, too, and together they would sometimes take walks by the creek or up onto the tops to look out across the valley. Her parents were tolerant of this friendship, keen that she should make a marriage from within the community.

"You've got time. Plenty of time. Both Leah and I got married early, it's not unusual to wait a while – certainly until after your rumspringa. Go to Philadelphia and enjoy yourself, then you'll see things more clearly," Alma said.

Miriam nodded. As much as she loved her two friends dearly, she had always felt like the younger sibling, talked down to at times, or presumed to be without the requisite wisdom an older woman might possess. The rumspringa was a chance to break free from that. To prove to herself and to others that she could take care of herself and make her own decisions. Both Alma and Leah had had the most unexpected of rumspringas, but Miriam was determined that hers would be a chance to experience something new and return to Faith's Creek confident in who she was and what she wanted.

"That's what I want. I want to find out more about myself, and decide what's right for me," Miriam replied, just as Jonathan Kemp came hurrying up to them across the farmyard.

"I'll see you later. I think Samuel might need changing," Alma said, and nodding to Jonathan, she walked off toward the barn.

"I'm not disturbing you, am I?" Jonathan asked.

Miriam shook her head. "Not at all, she's just giving us some space," she replied, smiling at him, as the two of them walked over to lean on the fence which ran along one side of the farmyard.

The wedding was being held at a farm just outside of Faith's Creek, where the barns were big enough to accommodate the ceremony and the celebration. But the other guests were already celebrating, and it was only Miriam and Jonathan who remained outside. The day was warm, the fields of corn stretching out toward the horizon, blowing gently in the breeze, and the scent of the harvest floated in the air.

"You look really nice today, Miriam," Jonathan said.

Miriam blushed. "It's a special day," she replied, flattered by his compliments.

The two of them had never spoken openly about their feelings, though there was something of an unspoken understanding between them. Theirs was a courtship without name, though the prospect of separation during Miriam's rumspringa loomed large. Jonathan had taken his own a year or so ago and had not stayed away long from Faith's Creek, preferring it to Philadelphia. He made his commitment to the community soon after returning.

"You always look nice," he said.

Feeling a flush of warmth, she smiled, gazing out toward the horizon, which at that moment seemed to represent the possibility of all that was to come. "You always say such nice things," she said.

Jonathan was a dependable sort, and though at times she allowed herself to ponder what might be if she were to meet another man, she knew that marriage to Jonathan was a very real possibility. There would be no question of her parents agreeing to it, and she wondered how Jonathan felt about her going away. They had not talked about it, though at times he had alluded to it. Now, the time was approaching, and she knew the conversation would soon arise.

"It's easy to say nice things to you," he said, putting his hand on her arm.

"You're always so kind..." she said, but he interrupted her, as though he had come to speak with her on a matter which was troubling him.

"Miriam... I... I need to talk to you. It's about your rumspringa. I know now's probably not the time..." he said.

She shook her head. "It's all right. I wanted to speak about it, too. We've avoided the subject long enough, haven't we?" she replied.

He nodded. "I'm going to miss you, it's hard... I want you to go and enjoy yourself, but... oh, I don't know, I'm sorry," he said.

Miriam slipped her hand into his and squeezed it. She did not want to hurt him, but neither did she intend to remain behind in Faith's Creek. The rumspringa was a rite of passage, a journey which all those of her age undertook. She had looked forward to it for many years, and she was certain that although it would be an adventure, it would be an adventure from which she would return.

"It's all right. Are you worried I might meet someone else?" she asked.

He nodded. "I know I'm not great at sharing my feelings. But I love you, Miriam, really, I do, and the thought of you... well, meeting someone else. It hurts," he replied.

His sentiment was sweet, and she smiled at him, hoping to reassure him. She was not ready to repeat his words – she had not known enough of the world to know if she was in love or not. But certainly, she had feelings for him. Feelings that were strong and growing stronger by the day.

"I'll miss you. I know I will. And I'm not going off to Philadelphia looking for someone else. I just want to see more of the world, to experience things I haven't known yet. When Leah and Alma came back from their rumspringa they were full of tales, not all of them good, I'll admit, but they'd had an adventure, and that's what I want, too," she said.

He sighed. "They had too much adventure," Jonathan said.

Miriam raised her eyebrows. "What do you mean?"

He shook his head. "The *bopplis*, all that trouble they got mixed up in. Leah got herself into a pretty dangerous situation, and as for Alma, she was going to jazz clubs and all sorts. I know they're your friends, but the rumors... a lot of people were talking," he said.

Miriam had not heard him speak like this before. She knew there had been talk in Faith's Creek about her friends – not all of it friendly – but that was in the past, and she was surprised at Jonathan for still harboring such prejudices.

"They did what was right by the *kinner*. Those two *bopplis* are better off here than where they'd be otherwise. Samuel would be in an orphanage, or with Sawyer struggling to make ends meet, and Elizabeth would be with those dreadful grandparents, the ones who mistreated her *mamm* so badly. How can you judge them?" she asked, pulling her hand away from Jonathan.

A dark scowl crossed his face. "I'm not judging them. I'm just telling you to be careful, that's all."

Miriam could not believe what he was saying. Did he not trust her, she wondered? He was acting strangely, as though her going away was an insult to him, and now she folded her arms and fixed him with a stern expression.

"I don't need to be told that. I can look after myself," she retorted.

Eyes widening, he gave her an incredulous look. "Is that so? Well, we'll see about that. Enjoy your time in Philadelphia, but just remember, I might not be here waiting when you get back!" With that, he turned on his heels and marched off across the farmyard.

Miriam watched him go, saddened by his words, which offered no ring of truth to them. She had no intention of chasing after other men and sighing to herself, she turned back toward the barn, determined to enjoy the wedding, even if Jonathan's words had left a sour taste in her mouth.

"Oh, hey there, Miriam," a voice called out, as she came to the barn door, and turning, she was faced by the one man she had not wished to encounter that day, Timothy Marshall. With a broad grin on his face, he stood waiting, it caused a spark of anger within her...

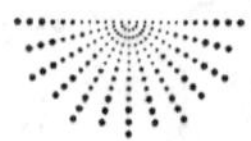

# CHAPTER TWO

Timothy Marshall was a gangly boy of seventeen, with light brown hair and hazel eyes. A small scar ran across his chin, the reminder of an accident involving hay bales as a child. He had always struck Miriam as an awkward individual, who laughed too much and rarely said the right thing.

Like Jonathan, he too had taken a shine to Miriam, and would often appear unexpectedly to speak with her. It was not that she wished to be rude, but Miriam found something about Timothy uncomfortable, and she tried to avoid him as best she could. She knew he had feelings for her – that much was clear – but there was nothing mutual in those feelings, and she would have preferred it if he simply left her alone.

"Timothy..." she said a little too sharply, edging toward the barn door.

"I've been wanting to talk to you all day. It's been a great wedding, huh?" he said.

Biting her lip, Miriam nodded. "They're so happy together. But I should..." she began, but he interrupted her.

"Only four days to go," he said, and she looked at him curiously, unsure of what he meant.

"Four days? I don't understand," she said, and he smiled at her.

"Until Philadelphia," he replied.

Miriam's heart sank.

She had forgotten his vague words of some previous months ago when he had told her he too was planning his rumspringa around the same time as hers. She had told him the date of her own departure out of politeness, never expecting that he would take it on himself to arrange for them both to coincide.

"You're going to Philadelphia on the same day as me?" she asked.

He nodded, still with a grin on his face. "Isn't it great? We can look round together, see the sights, eat out places, all of that," he said.

A sinking feeling almost dropped her to her knees, but all she could do was nod and force her expression into a smile. "How... lovely," she said.

"I can't wait to get out of Faith's Creek and see a bit more of the world. I feel like I've been missing out all this time, and to see it all with you, well, that's even better," he said.

She tried desperately to think of an excuse why the two of them could not share the experience together. "Well... I'm sure we might have a coffee together, or something. Philadelphia's a big place, and you're bound to find places you want to go yourself," she said, but still, his grin persisted.

"I'll be happy to go wherever you want to go," he replied.

It seemed Miriam would have no choice but to have Timothy tagging along at her side.

She excused herself from his company, explaining that she had promised to help take care of Elizabeth during the feast – which was not exactly a lie, but not entirely the truth, either.

"Were you talking to Timothy Marshall out there?" Alma asked as Miriam came to sit next to her.

"He was talking to me," she replied.

Alma smiled. "He's certainly got a flame for you," she said.

Miriam let out a groan. "That's what I'm afraid of," she said, thinking of Jonathan, and hoping he did not find out about her unwelcome tagalong.

It was two days before Miriam was due to set off on her rumspringa. She was making final preparations, her bags packed and ready, her tickets for the Greyhound bus laid out on the dressing table in her bedroom.

*Magical tickets to another world.*

Her *mamm* would pack sandwiches for her and a flask stood waiting to be filled so that it felt to Miriam as though she were stepping out on a grand adventure into the unknown, taking with her only what she needed, and leaving so much behind. Her *daed* had lectured her on her safety, reminding her of the dangers that a city like Philadelphia could present. He was only looking out for her, but Miriam was determined to make her own way, and if that meant mistakes, then so be it.

"I'm only telling you to be careful, that's all. You know what happened to your friends," her *daed* said, the look of concern so very plain in his old eyes.

Miriam groaned, when would they trust her. After all, what could go wrong?

# CHAPTER THREE

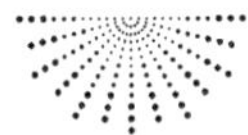

"For the last time, I won't come back with a *boppli*," she had replied, and her *daed* simply nodded.

Miriam looked down with satisfaction at her neatly ordered suitcases ready for her departure. She had not seen Jonathan since the day of the wedding, and she had avoided Timothy, too, hoping beyond hope he would not be on the bus with her, though nevertheless resigned to his company.

It pained her to think that Jonathan was upset, though she remained angry at the thought of his suspicions toward her. Miriam had no intention of betraying the trust between them, and certainly not with the likes of

Timothy Marshall, whose advances she had always resisted.

"Miriam, you've got visitors," her *mamm* called up the stairs, and she clattered down to the parlor, surprised to find Leah and Adam there.

They had brought Elizabeth with them, too, and Leah smiled, as Miriam's parents excused themselves.

"Why don't you both sit down," her *daed* said, and Miriam invited Leah and Adam to take chairs by the stove, pulling another from the dining table up for herself, as her *mamm* went to make coffee and her *daed* sat in his usual chair by the window.

"I was going to come to say goodbye before I left," Miriam said, as Leah and Adam glanced nervously at one another.

"We wanted to come and see you, it's such an adventure for you," Leah replied.

It seemed they had something on their mind, something which perhaps they would rather have spoken of without Miriam's *daed* sitting in the corner. Miriam's parents were strict and had always adhered to tradition. They were kind, but there was a line, one which Miriam never dared cross. They had made no secret of their suspicions over Adam – a convert to the Amish faith, and an outsider to the community, as far as they were concerned.

"How are you settling in, Adam?" Miriam's *daed* asked.

Adam had done much to ingratiate himself into the life of the community, and bit by bit, he was proving himself a dedicated convert. Bishop Beiler had welcomed him with open arms, but there were still some – like Miriam's parents – who remained suspicious.

"Very well, sir, thank you. I'm getting to grips with the farming and..." he began, but Miriam's *daed* interrupted him.

"That's good to hear, you've got a lot to learn," he said.

Miriam glanced at her daed and raised her eyebrows. "I'm sure Adam's more than capable, Daed," she said.

Her *daed* gave a curt nod. "It's not as easy as some people think," he replied.

Miriam's *daed* had been a farm laborer for many years, and her *mamm* did bookkeeping for others in the community. It was hard sometimes to make them understand other people's lives or to see beyond the boundaries of Faith's Creek. That was why Miriam was so pleased to be stepping out on her rumspringa – even though she knew she would come back, she knew too, she would be the richer for it.

"I'm a quick learner, sir, and I'm determined to settle in here and support my family," Adam said, putting his arm around Leah, who smiled.

"And you've done a great job of it so far," Leah replied looking up with such love in her eyes.

"But that's not why you came, is it?" Miriam asked.

Leah and Adam shook their heads. "No, it's something else..." Leah said, glancing at Miriam's *daed*, just as her *mamm* returned with the pot of coffee on a tray.

"Who wants coffee?" she asked, oblivious to the atmosphere that Leah's words had created.

"Leah's got something to tell us, Dawn," Miriam's *daed* said, and her *mamm* set down the coffee pot and looked at them curiously.

"Is that so?" she asked, glancing at Adam, her opinion of him being much the same as that of Miriam's daed.

"Look, Miriam, we're worried about you," Leah said.

Miriam furrowed her brow, puzzled at this sudden change in her friends.

Neither of them had expressed concern before, and she was not about to be lectured on the dangers of Philadelphia yet again.

"I can look after myself. I'm looking forward to going to Philadelphia," she said, but Leah shook her head and glanced at Adam, who took a deep breath.

"It's Jonathan Kemp, Miriam, there're things you should know about before you trust him too much," he said.

Miriam's eyes grew wide with astonishment. What could be wrong with Jonathan?

# CHAPTER FOUR

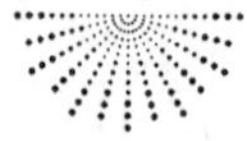

She had no idea that Adam knew anything about Jonathan. The two were merely acquainted, and she had barely confided her feelings for the man to Leah, preferring to wait until she was certain of what the future held. Now she shook her head, wondering whether she really wanted to know what Adam had to say, though her curiosity soon got the better of her.

"But what is it?" she asked, noting that her *mamm* was leaning closer determined to hear.

"Yes, I've never known Jonathan to be anything but a good and upstanding citizen," Miriam said, as Leah and Adam glanced at one another again.

"I'm sure he has his good points, but it's just..." Adam began, but now it was Miriam's *daed* who interrupted.

"I won't hear this talk, it's slander. What right have you to go about accusing a man of good heart and faith in such a way?" he demanded, rising angrily from his chair, and pointing his finger at Adam, who seemed somewhat taken aback.

"I was... we were..." he stammered.

"We were only trying to help. There are things you should know about Jonathan, things that might make you change your mind about pursuing things further," Leah said, looking imploringly at Miriam, who was unsure of what to do.

She knew nothing of any scandal surrounding Jonathan, nor of any reason why he should be considered an unsuitable match. He had been nothing but kind and gentle toward her, always eager to please, and a man of upstanding faith and morals. She had known him for many years and was certain that what she knew of him was the truth.

"Are you sure about this?" she asked, not wanting to doubt the sincerity of Leah and Adam's words but questioning whether perhaps they might be mistaken.

"We wouldn't have come if we weren't. We had to tell you," Leah said.

Miriam's daed was having none of it. "I won't hear this in my own home. I think it's time the two of you left. Coming here and corrupting my daughter like this," he growled.

"Wayne, please," Dawn said, but her *daed* shook his head.

"No, I know exactly what this is all about. They want Miriam to go off on her rumspringa and find herself a man, someone just like him," he said, pointing at Adam, who shook his head.

At the raised voices, Elizabeth had started to cry, Leah lifted her out of her carry basket and shushed her.

"It's all right," she said, but Elizabeth's wails now filled the parlor.

"I think you'd both better leave. I won't hear this kind of talk. Jonathan Kemp is a good man, an upstanding man, a man of good faith and morals. That's the kind of man I want my daughter to marry, not some outsider pretending to be part of our community, when in fact he has no idea of our values. I've heard enough. Don't you come by here anymore," he said, ushering Leah and Adam to the door.

"Wayne, where are your manners?" Dawn said, but her words fell on deaf ears, and Wayne was not satisfied until Leah and Adam were retreating along the garden path, Elizabeth's wails still echoing through the air.

"I won't have outsiders telling me what to do, or what's best for my daughter," he said, glaring angrily at Miriam and her *mamm*.

"But what do you suppose he meant by all of that? What has Jonathan done wrong?" Miriam asked.

She was curious to know the truth – more than curious. For the life of her, Miriam could think of nothing which would prevent her and Jonathan from marrying, if it were to be *Gott's* will, and the thought of some secret was almost too much to bear.

"He meant to cause trouble, that's what he meant to do," Wayne replied, and no amount of words from either Miriam or Dawn could convince him otherwise.

But Miriam was not about to accept that Leah and Adam's actions had been performed out of malice, and as the time for her to depart on her rumspringa approached, she grew more determined to know the truth, lest her feelings for Jonathan turned out to be a terrible mistake...

# CHAPTER FIVE

*A*fter further stern words from her *daed*, Miriam was hardly able to sleep that night, tossing and turning as she contemplated all she had learned – and those things she had not yet learned. Setting off on her rumspringa was supposed to be a fresh start, a chance to experience something new and different, but now Miriam felt as though she was about to leave unfinished business behind her – the cross words with Jonathan and the question of what Adam had intended to tell her. Her *daed* refused to allow her permission to visit with Leah and so Miriam would have no further opportunity to hear what Adam had to say – not until she returned from her rumspringa.

At the breakfast table that morning, the atmosphere was tense. Wayne offered only curt, cross words, and her *mamm*, though attempting to be reconciliatory, had sided with her *daed* in her opinion of Leah and Adam. As far as Miriam's parents were concerned, she should set her sights on marrying Jonathan and get over her rumspringa as soon as possible. But Miriam was unperturbed. The question of Jonathan loomed large for her, and she knew she needed to find some way of resolving it before she left for Philadelphia.

"I need to go to the market this morning, there're still a few things I need before I leave," she said, pushing aside her empty breakfast bowl.

"You're not going to see the Garretts, are you?" Wayne asked, and Miriam shook her head.

She knew how easily her *daed* could refuse her even now to go to Philadelphia, and she had no intention of jeopardizing that, however much she wanted to speak with Leah and Adam.

"I'll just go to the market and come straight back," she replied, rising from the table.

Wayne eyed her suspiciously, but he made no further comment, and she took up her shawl, bidding her parents goodbye before hurrying out of the house. She was glad to be away from the tense atmosphere which Leah and Adam's visit had created, the question of Jonathan hanging heavily in the air. As she walked, she pondered what it was that was so important that her friends had found it necessary to come and warn her, on the eve of her rumspringa.

"Miriam!" a voice behind her called out, and her heat sank, realizing that Timothy Marshall had just caught up with her.

"Hello, Timothy," she said, turning to find him grinning at her.

"All packed for the rumspringa?" he asked.

She nodded, not feeling the least bit in the mood for conversation. "I'm all ready," she said, trying to sound cheerful, though fearful of what he might say in reply.

"Me, too. I can't wait for us to get away from here," he said, still grinning at her.

The word "us" caused her to shudder, and she wished she had a more assertive nature – she could just imagine what Leah or Alma would say if one of them were here. But suddenly, a thought struck her, and she realized this encounter might prove providential. Timothy had a neighbor, a man named Samuel Philips. They both worked as laborers on one of the nearby farms, though Timothy had quit his job to go off on his rumspringa, and Samuel was a friend of Jonathan's. The two of them had traveled to Philadelphia for their rumspringa together, and if anyone might know something about Jonathan, then it was Samuel.

"Look, Timothy, there was something I wanted to ask you," Miriam said, adopting her most innocent tone.

"About us going away, you mean?" he replied, but Miriam shook her head.

"Your friend Samuel, he's a friend of Jonathan Kemp, isn't he?" she asked.

Timothy must surely have known something of Miriam's friendship with Jonathan, even if he considered himself to have the upper hand when it came to any future relationship. Miriam was not about to disabuse him of that belief, not if it meant learning the truth about Jonathan, and now Timothy looked at her in surprise and nodded.

"He knows him, sure, but what's the problem?" he asked.

"I was just wondering about Jonathan, that's all. I've heard some rumors, but I don't like to judge others, though I'd like to know the truth," she said.

"Rumors, what rumors?" he asked.

They were standing on the lane which led into Faith's Creek, and there was no one else about, only the swaying cornfields on either side. Miriam leaned forward, pretending she was taking Timothy into her confidence, and lowering her voice as she spoke.

"About women," she said, keeping it vague enough so as to suggest she knew something, even if she really knew nothing.

In truth, Miriam was not so concerned about the details concerning Jonathan's apparent misdemeanors, except, that is if they involved women. He had spoken so outrightly against her meeting other men in Philadelphia, that to discover he had had dalliances with other women would be to expose him as a hypocrite, and hypocrisy was one thing she detested above all else.

"Oh," Timothy replied, "yes, he's had a string of women."

At these words, Miriam's heart skipped a beat, and she stared at Timothy with wide-eyed astonishment.

"He has?" she asked.

Timothy nodded. "He and Samuel went off on their rumspringa together, and Samuel's told me all sorts of tales about what happened. And get this," he replied, leaning forward even further so that he and Miriam's faces were almost touching, "he still goes back."

Miriam startled, stepped back with an anguished cry, clutching her hand to her mouth.

"He still visits these women?" she exclaimed.

Timothy nodded. "That's what Samuel says. I don't know if it's true or not, but why would he lie?" Timothy asked, looking somewhat confused by Miriam's reaction.

"I don't think he would, it's just... it's a shock," she said, shaking her head as tears welled up in her eyes.

Miriam had not expected such a revelation. She had thought that the secrets Adam had learned could hardly be so bad as to totally alter her opinion of Jonathan – perhaps at times he took to the bottle or had been tardy in his work – all things she could easily forgive. She had come close to telling him she loved him, and now, she thanked *Gott*, she had not done so.

"I'm sorry, I didn't know you felt that way about him," Timothy said, suddenly looking hurt, and for the first time in her life, Miriam felt a twinge of guilt as to her behavior toward him, realizing her opinion of Jonathan had been totally wrong.

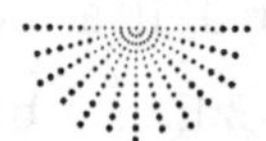

# CHAPTER SIX

Miriam felt broken by Timothy's words, but her anger was not against him, but against Jonathan, whose own words now meant nothing in the light of these extraordinary revelations. He had told her he loved her, and all the while he was going behind her back, slipping off to Philadelphia and to these nameless women. It seemed her *daed* had been right to warn her against the dangers of the city of brotherly love. She pulled a handkerchief from her pocket and dabbed the tears from her eyes.

Timothy looked at her with a confused expression. He seemed suddenly different, hurt by the realization of what he had now discovered.

"It's not your fault, Timothy. I asked you to tell me what you knew, and you told me," she said. Timothy nodded.

"I should have realized how you felt about him. It was obvious enough. I just... well, I care about you. I don't like seeing you hurt like this," he said.

Another pang of guilt ran through Miriam, who felt ashamed of the way in which she had treated Timothy in the past.

"I didn't feel... I wasn't sure. It's nothing against you, Timothy. But I need to know for certain. You see, it was Adam Garrett who told me about this, though my *daed* wouldn't hear him out. He sent him away before he could explain, and I didn't know what the truth was. I need to go and speak with him," she said, forgetting her *daed's* stern words forbidding her from doing just that.

"You mean you don't trust me to tell you the truth?" Timothy asked, sounding hurt.

"No, it's not that at all, but it was Adam who heard these rumors, too, or so I presume. Or perhaps he saw Jonathan in Philadelphia, oh... I don't know what to think," she exclaimed, unable to think clearly, a hundred questions going through her mind.

"I don't want anything bad to happen to you, Miriam. We've known one another all our lives. I know I can be a fool sometimes, but I'd never hurt you like that. I'm sorry it's not what you want to hear, but it's the truth. That's what Samuel told me. I was a fool not to realize you and Jonathan were... you know," he said, his words trailing off.

Miriam shook her head. In the past, she had found Timothy's attentions an annoyance, but now, despite the anguish, his words had caused her, she could not help but be grateful to him for his honesty in saving her from a terrible fate.

"We're not, that's not how it is. I like him... I liked him, but this... oh, it's too awful. But I must speak with Adam, not because I don't believe you, but because I need to know more," she said, taking hold of Timothy's hand and squeezing it.

He gave her a weak smile, though with a look of concern on his face, and she shook her head, realizing she was soon to learn further uncomfortable truths.

"Will you still go on your rumspringa?" he asked.

"Nothing would stop me, not even a pack of wild horses. We're going on that rumspringa, Timothy, and we'll enjoy ourselves," she replied.

Timothy's face brightened. "I'll pray for you, Miriam. I always pray for you, but I'll pray for *Gott's* guidance to help you through this and discover the truth," he said.

Thanking him, and with a new respect for the boy she had once thought a nuisance, Miriam hurried off toward Faith's Creek, determined to find answers to her questions.

THE CHICKENS WERE PECKING around at the front of the yard as Miriam opened the gate into Leah and Adam's smallholding. Despite her *daed's* opinion of him, Adam had proved an able smallholder, and the garden was filled with rows of neatly growing vegetables, edged all round with canes on which grew flowers for cutting, and rows of raspberry canes and redberry bushes. Miriam hurried up the steps and knocked loudly at the door. The sound of Elizabeth crying came from within, and a moment later, the door was opened and Leah looked out in surprise.

"Miriam, what are you doing here? Didn't your *daed* forbid..." she began, but Miriam interrupted her.

"He did, but I need to speak to you and Adam – about yesterday. I've found something out, and I don't care if my *daed* knows I've been here. I've got to know," she said.

Leah ushered her into the parlor, just as Adam emerged from the bedroom carrying Elizabeth in his arms.

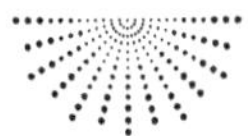

# CHAPTER SEVEN

The house was simply furnished, with just a few chairs set around the hearth, over which hung a large piece of embroidery given to the couple on their wedding day by Sarah Beiler. Leah invited Miriam to take a seat, she and Adam looking at her anxiously as without pause she explained what Timothy had told her.

"I'm afraid it's true," Adam said, shaking his head, as tears rolled down Miriam's cheeks.

Despite her words to Timothy, she had hardly dared believe that what he had told her was true. She had wanted the secret to be something else, anything but this.

"What do you know? How do you know?" she asked.

Adam glanced at Leah, who shook her head.

"Look, Miriam, you're upset, it's understandable. Here, why don't you hold Elizabeth, and I can make us some coffee," she said.

But Miriam was not in the mood to hold Elizabeth. She wanted answers, and now she demanded them from Adam.

"Just tell me what you know. Tell me what you were going to tell me yesterday. You can't keep it from me."

Adam nodded. "All right, Miriam. I want you to know the truth, but it's going to hurt. I can see you're hurting even now. Timothy wasn't lying to you. I've seen Jonathan in Philadelphia – on more than one occasion," he replied.

"On his own? But that doesn't prove anything..." she began.

Adam shook his head. "Not on his own, Miriam, with other women – different ones at different times. They wait for him at the bus depot, that's where I've seen him. I followed him once because I knew from Leah that the two of you were... well, you know," he said.

Miriam rolled her eyes. "We're not anything, but I thought we might have been something, that's all," she replied, wiping the tears from her eyes.

"Oh, Miriam, you poor thing," Leah said, and she came to put her arm around Miriam, who could not help but begin to sob.

"I'm sorry, I feel like such a fool, it's just that he told me so many things, he said so many things, and I believed him," she replied, dabbing at her eyes with a handkerchief.

"I can only tell you what I saw. He was with those other women, and they all seemed pretty happy in one another's company," Adam said.

"Do you think they know about one another?" Miriam asked, suddenly realizing she might not be the only woman for whom a startling revelation was to come.

"I wouldn't imagine so. If he can cheat on one, he can cheat on them all," Adam replied, and Leah nodded.

"You should have nothing more to do with him. We only wanted to warn you. We couldn't stand by and let you get hurt like that," Leah said.

Miriam gave them both a weak smile. "I know – it's like an Elastoplast. Sometimes you just have to pull it quickly off," she said.

Leah smiled. "It'll get better and knowing now will save a lot of pain to come," she said.

Miriam could only agree. As painful as it was, she knew that knowing the truth was better than living in the lie of Jonathan's creation. But what to do with her newfound knowledge was the next question. Should she confront him, or should she simply hold her head up high and reject any of his further advances?

"You're right. Maybe I've had a lucky escape," she replied.

AFTER BIDDING HER FRIENDS GOODBYE, and holding Elizabeth for the final time, Miriam began making her way home. Her route took her close to the home of Bishop Beiler and knowing what a help the Bishop's *fraa* had been to both Leah and Alma, Miriam decided to call on her. Her *daed* had called Jonathan a most upstanding man, a man of good morals and strong faith. But the revelations about him painted a very different picture, and Miriam could not help but wonder what others would think if they knew the truth.

"Oh, hello, Miriam, what can I do for you?" Sarah asked as she opened the door a few moments later.

"Can I talk to you about something?" Miriam asked.

Sarah invited her inside. The whole of Bishop Beiler's house felt like a library. The walls were lined with books in every room, broken only by the occasional picture or piece of furniture. The Bishop was not at home, and Sarah ushered Miriam into the kitchen, offering her coffee from a freshly brewed pot.

"I was just going to have one myself. Cookie?" she asked, offering Miriam a plate.

Miriam had always liked Sarah Beiler. She listened and never judged. Miriam felt as though she could tell her anything and she would know just the right thing to say in response.

"It's not easy to say this," Miriam began.

"Most important things aren't. Just tell me what's on your mind and we'll put the pieces together," she said, handing Miriam a cup of steaming coffee.

Miriam explained to Sarah all about her relationship with Jonathan, how they had been friends, and how that friendship had developed in the past few months. She told her how she had been flattered by his attentions and had no suspicions he was anything other than what she thought him to be, that is, until Leah and Adam had come to see her, and she had discovered the truth from Timothy. Sarah listened patiently, and there were times when Miriam had to pause to wipe a tear from her eye.

"I really trusted him, especially because it was he who questioned me over my fidelity," she said.

Sarah nodded. "I can understand why you're hurting, Miriam. It's a lot to discover in one day. Sometimes we think we know someone when actually, we don't. It's painful," she replied.

"I just don't know what to do. Do I confront him? Do I ignore him? Do I find out for myself?" Miriam asked.

Sarah pondered for a moment. "You need to follow your heart. Some people like to argue it out, some people just push their problems away, but if I know you, Miriam, you'll want to know the truth for yourself. Maybe you'll find it in Philadelphia," she replied.

"You know something, I think I might," Miriam replied, a plan forming in her mind, her sorrow eased by the thought that she might discover the truth for herself and lay to rest the fears which so held her back from finding the happiness she deserved.

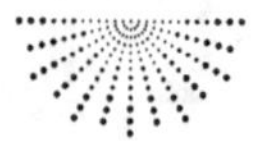

# CHAPTER EIGHT

Miriam's visit to Sarah Beiler had given her much to think on. With the final preparations for her rumspringa made, she was ready to leave Faith's Creek behind and go in search of the answers she desired. She had barely slept the night before, and though the tensions with her parents had eased, Miriam was still relieved when, at last, the time came to step out of the door on her adventure.

"I've made up your flask – hot coffee, and sandwiches, too," Dawn said, handing Miriam a packet that could easily have fed a dozen hungry travelers. There was a shake to her hand and moisture in her eyes.

"I'll be all right, *Mamm*. I've got the details for the hostel, and it's not like I'll be the only Amish woman in

Philadelphia. I'll make plenty of friends," she said.

Dawn nodded, more tears welling up in her eyes as she walked Miriam to the door, followed by Wayne, who gave her one final piece of advice.

"Just remember what's waiting for you when you get back here," he said.

Miriam nodded. She did not want to leave under a cloud. She was not shaking the dust from her feet, nor did she intend to stay away. Faith's Creek was her home, but she had waited for this moment long enough to know it was what she wanted. Now, she hoped that Philadelphia would also be the place where she found the answers she was seeking.

"I know that, *Daed*. It won't be long before I'm back, and I'm sure I'll be able to think more clearly about things then," she said.

Wayne smiled and pulled her into his arms, hugging her close one last time.

"You will soon be home," he said, and he kissed her cheek before he and Dawn walked her down the porch steps and across the garden.

"You've got plenty of handkerchiefs, haven't you?" Dawn asked.

Miriam smiled. "Two dozen – two dozen more than I need. Don't worry, *Mamm*, I'll be all right," she said kissing them both goodbye. It felt so close to freedom as she stepped out of the gate to walk along the lane toward the bus stop. Her breath was held as if some force may pull her back.

Pausing, she turned to wave to them, and at last, it felt as though she were breaking free. Miriam loved her parents dearly, but she knew the time had come to make her own way in the world. To discover the person she was meant to be. This would be quite an adventure, one which she had looked forward to for so long, and that was now happening. As she turned, she took a deep breath knowing that there could be no going back – this was her rumspringa and she prayed to *Gott* that it would provide her with the many answers she sought.

"Miriam!" a familiar voice called out, and turning, she found Timothy hurrying toward her, a large suitcase in hand and a smile on his face.

Mixed emotions went through her but she knew she had to let this happen however, it did.

* * *

"This sure is exciting, isn't it?" Timothy said, gazing out of the window.

He was sitting in front of Miriam, his nose pressed to the glass, as the bus sped across the wide-open prairie land toward Philadelphia. Miriam could not help but smile at his eagerness, she was also excited at the prospect of what was to come. In truth, Timothy was not a bad traveling companion, particularly given what they had now shared.

"I'm looking forward to seeing the big city," she said.

His eyes opened wide and seemed to shine in his face. "About all that stuff the other day. I'm sorry if it upset you. I didn't mean it to. It's just... well, I hope you know it's the truth," he said.

She nodded. "Actually, I know it is. I went to see Adam. He told me the same thing. He'd seen Jonathan in Philadelphia with other women, and that confirmed what you told me. I'm the one who should be apologizing. I didn't want to believe it, but I know you were only telling me the truth," she said.

His eyes dimmed and his mouth turned down. "I wouldn't do anything to hurt you, Miriam. You know I wouldn't," he said.

"I know that. But I need to know for certain. At the moment, we only have Samuel's and Adam's word for it. I need to know... to see for myself. I didn't want to ask Jonathan – he might tell me anything or make something up – he might lie to me! I need to find out for myself, and I think I'll find those answers in Philadelphia," she said.

Miriam had thought long and hard about what to do. She wanted to give Jonathan a chance – as much as the thought of what he had done caused her upset. There was still the possibility of confusion, and that both Samuel and Adam could be wrong – though it seemed unlikely. She intended to make some inquiries in Philadelphia and, if she could, discover the truth.

"And what if what you find out isn't very nice?" Timothy asked.

Miriam sighed. "Well, I'll just have to accept that, won't I?" she replied, as the suburbs of the city came into view. But could she? How would it feel if all Jonathan had said to her was a lie?

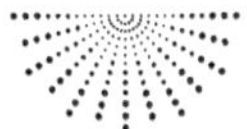

# CHAPTER NINE

After her quiet upbringing in Faith's Creek, arriving in Philadelphia was a shock to the senses. Miriam could not believe the number of people milling about the bus depot, nor the hustle and bustle of the street, down which she and Timothy now fought their way, carrying their bags with them.

"The hostel is on Blake Street, it's the same one Alma stayed at when she came on her rumspringa," Miriam said, peering down at the instructions she had with her. They had seemed so simple back home, now they were like a foreign language written upside down in a doctor's handwriting.

"But where's Blake Street?" Timothy replied.

Miriam shrugged. "I don't know – I didn't expect it to be... well, like this," she said, feeling quite overwhelmed by the enormity of the city, which seemed to loom down on them like some terrible beast.

It was overwhelming, and Miriam was glad when Timothy suggested they step into a coffee shop and make inquiries.

"Macchiato, Mocha, Cortado, Americano, Ristretto. You name it," the bearded barista behind the counter said when Miriam asked what kind of coffee they served.

"Oh... I don't know, just normal," she said, never having heard of such bizarre choices.

"Black?" the barista replied, sounding slightly disappointed at not being able to show off his skills.

"Two black coffees," Miriam replied, thankful to have finally understood, and glancing at Timothy, who appeared equally out of his depth.

"New in town? You're Amish, aren't you?" the barista asked, and Miriam nodded her kapp and shawl, and Timothy's plain clothing and straw hat being perhaps the best giveaway.

"We just arrived, we're on our rumspringa," Miriam replied, as the barista placed the two cups of coffee down on the counter.

"We get a lot of Amish in here. They all look like you at first – nervous. But you'll soon settle in," he said, smiling at them both.

"Say, you don't happen to know where Blake Street is?" Miriam asked.

The barista nodded. "Finish your drink and I'll point you in the right direction," he replied.

Miriam was grateful to at last be finding her feet.

With the barista's directions, the hostel was not hard to find, and it seemed like an oasis of calm in comparison to the chaos of the city all around. Miriam set down her bags in the large entrance hall of what had once been a warehouse. It was now converted into three floors of dormitories. She had never spent a night away from home before, and everything seemed strange and unfamiliar. A woman behind the counter greeted them, already having their names and addresses. With a fixed smile she directed them to their respective dormitories. Miriam and Timothy agreed to meet back in the entrance hall, which also served as a communal seating area.

"I won't be long," she said, and he nodded, picking up his suitcase and disappearing through a doorway marked, "Men's Dormitory."

The woman's dormitory lay at the top of a flight of stairs on the third floor, with mixed dormitories on the middle floor. Miriam heaved her suitcase up the stairs, pausing breathlessly at the top. It had been quite a day, filled with new sights and people. Despite all her anticipation, she had not been ready for the fast pace of the city. It was such a contrast to all she had known before.

"Rumspringa?" a woman in the dormitory asked, as Miriam entered a few moments later.

She was a few years older than Miriam, her dark hair combed back and tied in a ponytail, and a smile on her face, which was pretty. Despite having no kapp, her clothes were simple, and Miriam wondered if she too had come from the Amish community.

"That's right, I just arrived from Faith's Creek," she said.

The woman smiled. "Oh, I know Faith's Creek. I've met the Bishop's *fraa*, Sarah Beiler. You must know her," she said.

Miriam smiled, realizing that Philadelphia was not as big as she might first have thought.

The woman's name was Sandra, and after exchanging further pleasantries, Miriam made her way back down to the entrance hall, where she found Timothy reading a guidebook to Philadelphia. He looked up at her and smiled. He had changed his shirt, and removed his hat, dressed, it seemed, like a man from the city, rather than an Amish man from the country.

"I'm reading about an ice cream parlor we should try. They have fifty different flavors. Do you think we could try them all?" he said.

Miriam smiled. "We could try," she replied. "I think we would be sick though."

It surprised her just how much she was warming to Timothy. He was kind and considerate, with good morals, and a sense of humor, too. He did not take himself too seriously, but he had been there for her when she was hurting, and now it seemed he would be loyal to her in her search for the truth.

"And there's this burger place I've found. But it does footlongs, too. I could eat it all," he said.

Miriam laughed. "You're like a *kinner* in a candy store," she said.

The grin on his face certainly fit that description. "I'm just pleased to be seeing a bit of the world..." he said, just as the cries of a *boppli* cause them both to look up.

A woman was coming down the stairs, dragging several suitcases with her, and holding a *boppli* in her arms. She was young, perhaps twenty years old, and dressed in a flower-patterned skirt and blouse. Miriam smiled to see the child, but her smile soon disappeared at the sound of the woman's voice.

"Oh, little George Kemp, will you stop your wailing," she cried.

Miriam's heart froze as she and Timothy looked at one another in amazement. It couldn't be... could it?

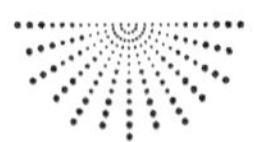

The coincidence of the boppli's name seemed too much to ignore. Miriam rose to her feet, hurrying to help the woman, who was struggling with her suitcases.

"Here, let me help you," she said.

The woman looked up and smiled. "Oh, would you?" she asked, holding out the *boppli* for Miriam to take.

She seemed unperturbed at handing the child over to a complete stranger, but Miriam was well used to *bopplis*, and she took him in her arms and rocked him back and forth, whilst Timothy took the woman's suitcases in hand.

"Are you leaving?" Miriam asked.

The woman nodded, her smile dropping, her face so sad. "We are, but it's not easy with a *boppli* in tow. Not that we'll get any help from his *daed*, that is," she said, and by her accent and turn of phrase, Miriam knew the woman was Amish.

"We're from Faith's Creek. My name's Miriam. This is Timothy," she said.

The woman looked at them in surprise. "Faith's Creek? Now there's a surprise," she said.

Miriam knew she had to ask the question. "I couldn't help overhearing you call George by his surname, too, Kemp. I know a Kemp, Jonathan Kemp," she said, trying to sound as casual as possible, but desperate to know the connection, as much as she feared the answer.

The woman nodded – it really was a small world, after all.

"I know Jonathan Kemp," she replied, "I know him very well."

"Why don't you come and sit down. If you've got time, that is?" Timothy said.

The woman nodded.

They sat by a large bay window which looked out onto the gardens behind the hostel, and through which the sun streamed, flanked by pot plants. It was secluded, and out of hearing from anyone else. George was happily playing on the rug.

"I'm Robyn Crocker, a native of a town downstate, some fifty miles from Faith's Creek. I've been trying to make my way in the world as a waitress, though it's hardly worked out well. I get a job, then I can't hold it down. It's hard having a *boppli* to look after on your own," she said, shaking her head.

"But you know Jonathan because..." Miriam asked.

Robyn shook her head. "Because he's George's *daed,* of course. Not that he ever shows up to help. He's a liar and a cheat, and I don't want anything to do with him. I might even stop calling George by the name, though that's what he's registered as, and I suppose it fits," she said, glancing down at her son, who now rolled onto his back and gurgled.

"He's a beautiful boy," Miriam said, trying hard not to show her emotions.

This chance encounter proved what she was seeking. Jonathan was just as Samuel and Adam had said he was, and it pained her to think of Robyn – and goodness knows who else – being hurt by him in such a way. She felt angry at Jonathan, angry that he could behave like this and get away with it. How could he leave such a trail of destruction behind him?

"He's a blessing. I always say that. Whatever I feel about his *daed*, I know we brought something precious into the world. Though I feel sad George won't ever know him, and he'll never know George. I tried to keep in touch, I tried to talk to him, but it was like talking to a brick wall. He wanted nothing to do with George, or with me. I know he had other women, but it still hurts," she said.

Miriam nodded.

She was not ready to reveal to Robyn that she, too, had been one of those women, but she knew just how Robyn must feel. Robyn looked exhausted, and it seemed she was at her wit's end as to what to do next.

"You've been through a lot," she said.

Robyn nodded. "I don't know what we'll do. I'm thinking about going out west to look for work. I always wanted to be an actress, but it hardly pays the bills. I've got nothing," she said, and a tear rolled down her cheek.

Miriam's heart went out to her. She was trying her best, but her best would not put food on the table or provide daycare for George. Jonathan had abandoned her, and for a moment, Miriam saw a terrible vision of what her own fate might have been had she ignored the warnings from Adam and Timothy. She glanced at Timothy, who shook his head, a grave expression on his face.

"I can't believe any man could treat a woman like that," he said, shaking his head.

"Well, believe it," Robyn said, shrugging her shoulders.

She seemed resigned to a life of hardship, accepting of her lot, but Miriam wondered if there might be a way of helping her – at least for a short while.

"What if I were to look after George while you find work out west? I could take care of him, I'm good with *bopplis* – I've looked after several. I could take care of him, and you could get yourself established in a new job. I know it might sound crazy, but..." she said, hardly knowing what she was saying, but feeling it was the right thing to say at that moment. Her words felt like a gift of inspiration from *Gott*.

She expected Robyn to refuse immediately. The idea was too incredible, but to her surprise, Robyn breathed a sigh of relief.

"You'd do that? You'd take care of him for me? I don't know what to say," she said.

Timothy interrupted. "Miriam, are you sure about this? It's a big responsibility," he said.

Miriam nodded. "I know what I'm doing, Timothy. I'd love him as my own. It would only be for a short while, just until Robyn got herself sorted. She can't take care of George and hold down a job, but once she's established…" Miriam said, glancing at Robyn, who nodded.

"I've been finding it hard to cope. I've had to, but it's been hard. I love George with all my heart, but I can't take care of him and find a job at the same time. It's just not possible," she said, and Timothy nodded.

"Would we take him back to Faith's Creek?" he asked, and at this, Robyn's expression changed.

"I don't want Jonathan anywhere near him. You wouldn't let him see him, would you?" she asked, looking anxiously at Miriam, who shook her head.

Now, it seemed, was the time, to tell the truth, and she explained to Robyn why she was so anxious to help her.

"So, I do understand," she said, as her explanation came to an end, and Robyn sighed.

"What a swine he is. Did he tell you he loved you?" Robyn asked, and Miriam nodded.

"I'm just glad I didn't say it back. When I look at you, I think how close I came to being just the same. My parents think he's the most upright of men – the whole community does. But he's got some secrets, and I'm sure George isn't the only one," Miriam replied, shaking her head.

"And you promise he won't go anywhere near George?" Robyn asked.

Miriam promised. "I won't tell him. But I'll take good care of your *boppli*, I promise," she said, and to her surprise, Timothy expressed the same sentiments.

"And I'll step up, too. We'll both look after George, and when you've found work, we'll bring him back to you. We'll write to you every day, you'll know everything that happens," he said.

Robyn smiled. "It's a burden off my back. You're both very kind, and I know you'll look after George," she said, reaching down to pick up the *boppli* from the rug.

She kissed him and handed him over to Miriam.

"I'll take good care of him, and once you've got yourself settled, we'll bring him to you," she said, as Robyn brushed a tear from her eyes.

"Everything you'll need is in this bag," she said, handing one of her suitcases over to Timothy, who smiled at her reassuringly.

"You'll see him again before you know it," he replied.

Robyn nodded, patting George on the head and kissing him again. "Be a good boy," she said, and with a final glance at them, she hurried out of the hostel.

Miriam stood with George in her arms, astonished at what had just happened. It had all happened so quickly, and to think that she was now responsible for the *boppli* she held was quite incredible. She looked up at Timothy, who appeared equally bemused, the two of them shaking their heads, as George began to cry.

"Can I do this?" Miriam asked.

Timothy shook his head. "No, but we can," he said, smiling at her, and putting his arm around them both.

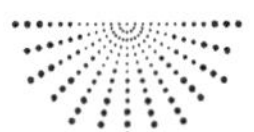

# CHAPTER ELEVEN

*H*aving vowed not to end up like either Leah or Alma, Miriam now found herself unexpectedly the *mamm* of a *boppli*. It had not been planned, nor had she ever imagined that Robyn would agree to the idea. But it seemed *Gott* had a plan for her, and Miriam was willing to trust that her chance encounter with another of Jonathan's former lovers was a sign she was doing the right thing. She had come to Philadelphia hoping to discover the truth, and the truth had found her.

Miriam and Timothy settled into the hostel with George, the proprietor being kind enough to assign Miriam a private room – if only for the sake of the other guests. George could be demanding, and he often cried, much to Miriam's distress. She had often taken care of Elizabeth and Samuel back in Faith's Creek, but there she was able to hand the *bopplis* back to their respective *mamms*. Here Miriam was George's *mamm*, and she had no choice but to take care of him as best she could.

"Oh, more diapers, that's what we need. And would you get me some chocolate?" Miriam asked as she stood holding George in her arms.

Timothy was sitting at the desk in Miriam's room by the window, scribbling down a list, and he nodded, glancing up at her with a smile.

"Won't he settle?" he asked.

Miriam shook her head.

George had been awake for most of the night, tossing and turning in his cot, and crying incessantly. Miriam had tried everything to quieten him, but to no avail, and she was close to her wit's end, desperate to do what was right – but not knowing what that was. Taking care of a *boppli* was such an enormous responsibility, and Miriam was feeling increasingly overwhelmed by what she had taken on. She loved George, for she felt a special sense of responsibility toward him, and wanted to do her best by him, honoring her promise to Robyn.

"I don't know what to do. He's so hard to settle," she said, bouncing George up and down in her arms.

"I tell you what, why don't you do the shopping, and let me look after him for a while?" Timothy said.

Miriam looked at him in surprise. She had not expected him to offer, though there was no reason why he should not. Timothy had been diligent in taking care of them both and had gone above and beyond in his duty and loyalty. This was just another example of him proving himself far more than the man she had thought him to be.

"All right, if you're sure," she said, handing the screaming baby over to Timothy, who rocked him back and forth in his arms, whispering something in his ear, and smiling.

"There now, it's all right. You were just having a good cry, weren't you? We all need that sometimes. There're days I wish I could just scream like that. It would make me feel a lot better. That's it, you're fine, aren't you?" he said, and Miriam had to smile at the sight of Timothy playing *daed* with George.

He was a natural, and George was soon settled in his cot, next to which Timothy kneeled, rocking him gently back and forth.

"Are you sure you'll be all right?" Miriam asked.

Timothy nodded. "I think we'll be just fine," he said.

Miriam took up the list and slipped quietly out of the room.

She was impressed by how Timothy had stepped up. He had done a lot of growing up in the weeks since they had arrived in Philadelphia. Although strange circumstances had forced them more closely together than Miriam could ever have imagined, she was far from unhappy at being in his company. Timothy had proved himself, and in contrast to Jonathan, there could be no question of which man possessed the better morals and the kindest heart. She pondered this as she made her way to the store, now feeling quite at home in Philadelphia, even if her rumspringa had not worked out in quite the way she had planned.

"I GOT a whole load of diapers and... oh," Miriam said, as she entered her room at the hostel an hour or so later.

Timothy was sitting in a chair by the window with George in his arms. They were both asleep, though at the sound of the opening door, Timothy stirred, opening his eyes and yawning.

"Oh, did I fall asleep?" he said.

Miriam smiled warmed by the sight of them. "More importantly, George did," she replied, pointing to the sleeping *boppli*.

Timothy nodded. "I'm glad I can do something right," he said, rising to his feet and placing George gently into his crib.

"You do a lot that's right, Timothy," Miriam said, setting down her bags of shopping and smiling at him.

"I always wanted *kinner*. It sounds foolish, I know, but I always dreamed about having a family. I'd be a good *daed*, I know I would," he said.

Miriam nodded. "I think you would – I know you would. I can see it now. I know we're struggling, and this isn't exactly how either of us thought our rumspringa would turn out, but... well, we're doing all right, aren't we?" she said.

Timothy nodded. "I'd say we're doing pretty well," he replied.

Miriam stepped forward and slipped her hand into his. She felt at ease with him, their shared experience had brought them closer together. Where once she had seen a man she barely liked, she now saw a man she could barely live without. It was a strange feeling, one which had come over her quite suddenly, but one she was not about to fight. He blushed, looking down at her and smiling.

"I misjudged you, Timothy. Back in Faith's Creek things were different. We've done a lot of growing up these past few weeks, and I couldn't have done this without you, really, I couldn't," she said.

"I'm just happy to be here, I'm happy to be with you and George, but..." he began, and his words trailed off.

"But what?" she asked, and he sighed.

"But I don't know what we'll do next. We can't stay here much longer – it's not exactly the rumspringa either of us had in mind, is it? What's going to happen when we get back to Faith's Creek with a *boppli* in tow? What will your parents say?" he asked.

Miriam had tried not to think about this inevitability. But Timothy was right, they could not stay in Philadelphia forever, and returning to Faith's Creek would present a whole new set of challenges for them both. Miriam had not told her parents about George, and in her letters home she had merely spoken of the delights of Philadelphia – the ice cream parlor, the coffee shops, the municipal parks – and all the fun she was having. It would be a very different story when she stepped off the bus and returned home. But Miriam was adamant she had done the right thing in offering to care for George, and with Timothy's help, she was certain she would succeed in persuading those back home she was fit to be his *mamm*.

"We'll see what they say. I know it won't be favorable, but... well, you'll be there, won't you?" she asked.

Timothy nodded. "I'm not going anywhere, I promise," he replied, and unlike Jonathan's empty words, Miriam knew she could trust everything Timothy told her.

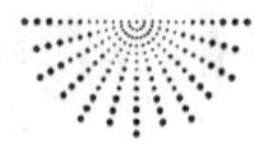

# CHAPTER TWELVE

In the days that followed, Miriam found herself thinking more and more about their return to Faith's Creek. Her *mamm* and *daed* would never accept George as her own – however much she pleaded. She could hear the anger in her *daed's* voice and see the disappointment on her *mamm's* face. It would be too much to bear, and despite having Timothy at her side, she was coming to dread the inevitability of what was to come. She wondered if there could be another way, and by the time she and Timothy were due to leave Philadelphia, Miriam's mind was made up.

"We need to talk about what's going to happen," she said, two days before the date of their departure.

"I've been thinking about it, too," Timothy admitted, as the two of them walked with George by the lake in the nearby park.

It was a beautiful summer day, and the city was busy with people enjoying the sunshine. They had taken George to the ice cream parlor and sat with coffee and cake at their favorite café. It had been an idyllic afternoon, and Miriam was loath to leave it all behind, knowing what it was they were returning to. Despite her earlier insistence that Faith's Creek was the right place for her, she had not counted on returning under such unusual circumstances, and now that the time had come, the thought of it terrified her.

"I don't know what my *mamm* and *daed* will say when I walk through the door with George," she said, shaking her head.

She had thought long and hard about it, and none of the possible scenarios ended well. Her parents would almost certainly forbid her from keeping George. They would tell her she was too young, and that he was the responsibility of his *mamm*. Miriam had written every day to Robyn, assuring her that George was happy and well looked after. Robyn would write back to them each week and had now found herself a job at a theater out west.

She was saving money for a deposit on an apartment. She was happy, but Miriam knew she missed George terribly.

"I don't think they'll be too pleased about it," Timothy replied.

"That's why I think we need to do something different. We can't go back to Faith's Creek, not yet," she said, taking a deep breath.

She was nervous, for she had not yet broached her idea with him and was anxious as to what he might say.

"What then?" he asked, looking at her in surprise.

"We don't go back, not yet, at least," she replied, glancing at him nervously.

The idea had come to her some days previously while she prayed, and at first, it had seemed crazy – though no crazier than taking on another woman's *boppli* on a whim. Instead of returning to Faith's Creek, she and Timothy would go to a rural area on the cusp of the Pocono mountains. She would tell her parents she was traveling and not yet ready to return home. They would remain there for nine months before returning to Faith's Creek as husband and *fraa* – George being the product of their union. It was an extraordinary idea, but the thought of marrying Timothy had taken on fresh appeal during the time they had spent together in Philadelphia. Miriam knew he would marry her, and she had come to know him well enough to realize her feelings for him were growing.

"Then when do we go back?" he asked.

Miriam smiled. "In nine months, just long enough to be married and for a child to be born," she replied.

Timothy stared at her in amazement.

Miriam was surprised at how little persuasion was required to have Timothy agree to her plan – in fact, he took to it readily. The idea of marriage was something she had thought to be a long way off. Her intention had been to return to Faith's Creek and find a man to fall in love with. At first, Miriam had believed that man would be Jonathan, but now, following the terrible revelations about him, she knew she could never again look him in the face, let alone trust him.

Back in Faith's Creek, Miriam would never have chosen Timothy, but in Philadelphia, he had more than proven himself. In her heart, she knew that her feelings for him were growing stronger by the day. It was not the ideal basis for marriage, and she could only imagine the horror with which her parents would react if they knew the truth, but Miriam was adamant she was old enough to make up her own mind. Old enough to take care of George, and that meant finding a way to keep him safe and avoid the possibility of his being taken away.

"I'll miss the ice cream parlor," Timothy said, as he carried Miriam's suitcases down from her room at the hostel.

"There might be one in Pocono," she replied.

"So long as we're together, that's all that matters," he said, and she nodded.

They intended to get married in the coming week and would go to the court house to perform the ceremony, just the two of them and George. It was not the wedding Miriam had envisioned, but it would be good enough, and ensure that in nine months, when they returned to Faith's Creek, they would go home respectably.

"I've got a feeling Robyn won't take George back," she said after they had settled up their bill and bid the hostel proprietor farewell.

They were walking toward the bus depot, and Miriam was carrying George in a sling across her back, while Timothy hauled their suitcases along next to her.

"What makes you say that? She dotes on him," he replied.

Miriam shook her head. Robyn's letters had become less frequent, and though Miriam had been diligent in keeping George's *mamm* up to date with their intentions – including the move to Pocono – it seemed there was little interest on Robyn's part in why Miriam and Timothy should be going to such lengths.

"But I think she's realized she can't take care of him. She can't be the *mamm* he needs. Not in her circumstances. She loves him, but she knows he's better with us," Miriam replied.

Miriam was unsure whether she believed her own words. But she had been surprised by Robyn's recent lack of interest in George. It was as though she had real-ized just how hard it had been to find herself alone with a *boppli*. Miriam was glad she had been there to help in Robyn's hour of need, and now she wanted to ensure that when she returned to Faith's Creek with George, her family would accept him.

"I won't argue with that," Timothy replied, as they arrived at the bus depot.

There was a bus leaving for Pocono in around half an hour, and another, which would have taken them to Faith's Creek. Miriam felt as though she were at a crossroads, and despite praying to *Gott* for guidance, she knew her mind was already made up. This was surely *Gott's* will for her, and she was determined to do all she could to protect George and ensure they could be a family together.

"Here goes nothing," she said, as they stepped onto the bus heading for Pocono.

Timothy took her by the hand and smiled. "It's a new adventure – isn't that what a rumspringa's all about?" he replied, just as George began to cry.

# CHAPTER THIRTEEN

They had managed to find a pastor to officiate. It made it a little better than using a judge, though it was nothing like the wedding they would have back home.

"And do you, Miriam Dawn Graber, take this man to be your lawfully wedded husband," the pastor asked.

"I do," Miriam replied with a lump in her throat. She had butterflies in her stomach from fear, joy, and the enormity of the step she was taking. Once this was done there was no turning back.

There had been no difficulty in finding a place to marry when they had arrived in Pocono. Miriam had simply stated that her parents would only accept the baby if she and Timothy were married – a truth, though not the full truth. Few questions had been asked, and now they were standing in a stark, whitewashed room together, in front of a man in a suit and next to the state and national flags, making their vows. Two witnesses had been found, and now the pastor pronounced them man and wife.

"You may kiss the bride," he said.

Timothy turned to Miriam and smiled. "Congratulations," he whispered, leaning forward and kissing her somewhat awkwardly.

It was the first kiss they had shared, and the sensation was strange, though not unpleasant. She smiled at him, slipping her hand into his, as the pastor and witnesses offered their congratulations.

"But didn't you have any family you wanted here, too?" the pastor asked.

He reminded her of her *daed*. They were around the same age, each with graying black hair and bushy eyebrows. Miriam blushed and shook her head.

"It's the bop... baby, you see, my parents wouldn't approve. But we wanted to do the right thing," she said.

The pastor smiled. "I understand," he said, ushering them out of the room so that the next couple might make their vows.

"It's a shame you can't have any prayers at a civil ceremony," Miriam said, as she and Timothy walked down the street in Pocono to their lodgings.

They had brought a stroller for George, and he was fast asleep in it, his thumb in his mouth. A feeling of love enveloped her as she looked down at him and smiled, grateful at last to be a family, albeit in the strangest of circumstances. Her rumspringa had hardly been what she had intended, but then it fell within the tradition of her two friends Leah and Alma – the irony of which was not lost on Miriam. Both of them had gone to Philadelphia with certain expectations, only to have them turned upside down by the appearance of an unexpected *boppli*. Miriam had promised herself that would not happen to her, but here she was, marrying a man she had not intended to, and with a *boppli* that was not even hers.

"We can pray ourselves, it's surely *Gott's* will," Timothy replied, slipping his hand into hers.

Miriam had come to trust more readily in *Gott* these past few months. It was *Gott's* will she should take care of

George, and *Gott's* will that had brought her and Timothy together. There were many questions still to be answered. Miriam had not even told Leah or Alma of her marriage, let alone her parents. But in all of this, in all the confusion, and with all the questions still to be answered, one thing was certain, Miriam knew she had done the right thing.

"Home sweet home for the next nine months," Miriam said, looking around their simple lodgings a few moments later.

It lay on the edge of the town, looking out over a forest, a small bungalow with just a lounge and bedroom, a small galley kitchen, and a shower room built. It was a far cry from Miriam's home in Faith's Creek, but it was comfortable enough, and now they were married, Timothy no longer had to sleep on the settee.

"I just hope I can get work soon. I'll try Walmart, and a couple of the stores tomorrow. They might have a warehouse position going," Timothy said, as Miriam lifted George out of his stroller.

"We'll be all right," Miriam said, though she knew their savings were running low.

All they had to do was get through the next nine months. Her parents believed they were traveling around the state, and Miriam would continue writing letters to reassure them she was safe. They would be surprised to find her married – but they could hardly object, for Timothy was a good and upstanding man, a man of principles and morals. No one in Faith's Creek could possibly object to the match, could they? Miriam knew of one person she did want to tell and when George was settled down for the night, she took up pen and paper and wrote a long letter to Sarah Beiler informing her of everything that had happened. The Bishop's *fraa* was the only one whom Miriam was certain would understand. She would not judge nor chastise but accept they had done the right thing. Of that, Miriam was certain.

"Are you happy?" Timothy asked when later that evening they had eaten a simple supper and laid George down in his crib to sleep.

"I am," she replied, reaching across the table and taking him by the hand.

Their life was simple and far different from anything she had ever imagined. But Miriam had a family, a husband who loved her, and a *boppli* that she loved beyond measure. There was little else she desired, and she was grateful to Timothy for all he had done. She knew that whatever happened, they would have one another for better or worse.

# CHAPTER FOURTEEN

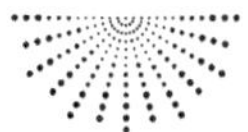

Timothy had some good fortune the following day. The Walmart in Pocono was hiring, and he secured employment in the warehouse. It was not much, but the wage would be enough to support them both, while Miriam took care of George. It seemed that yet again, *Gott's* providence was watching over them.

Miriam began to think nine months in Pocono would not be so bad, after all. Their neighbors were pleasant, an elderly couple – the Jenkinsons – who doted on the sight of George. Mrs. Jenkinson even found some mending for Miriam to take care of, and after a few weeks, she had several dozen women bringing her things to mend and some for clothes to make.

"You need something to keep your mind occupied. Babies make you forget everything," Mrs. Jenkinson told her, and Miriam was grateful to her – not only for the advice but for the work, too.

"Things have turned out all right," Miriam said, as she and Timothy sat at the table eating dinner a few weeks after their arrival in Pocono.

George was playing on the rug. He had grown so much bigger since they had left Philadelphia, and it seemed that every week Miriam was having to find new clothes for him to wear.

"We might not want to leave," Timothy replied, smiling at her as she spooned out a dish of buttered noodles for him.

"I miss it, though. I like Pocono well enough, it's pretty here, but... I'll be glad to be home," she said.

"I know what you mean, if this rumspringa's taught me anything, it's that I like a simple way of life. I want to go back to laboring on the farm, maybe have a smallholding, a little house to call my own – I don't want much," he said.

Miriam smiled at him. "And will you want a *fraa* when you're back in Faith's Creek?" she asked.

He paused, lowering his fork, and nodded. "Aren't you my *fraa*?" he replied.

"I'm glad I am," she said.

It had taken a while to get used to the idea. Back in Faith's Creek, Miriam had been adamant she would never marry Timothy. But things change, people change, and in discovering the truth about Jonathan, she had learned the truth about Timothy, too. He was not the man she had believed him to be – far from it. Wishing for nothing more to do with Jonathan, Miriam was only too glad to be married to a man like Timothy, a man who cared for her, and whom she had grown to love.

"You know, I wish we'd been married in different circumstances. You deserved more than a courthouse wedding. We should have been married in Faith's Creek, with all our family and friends around us. Just like Leah and Adam, and Alma and Sawyer. Those were happy days. Maybe when all this has calmed down we could do that, have Bishop Beiler bless us, and do things properly," he said, tucking into his noodles.

"I'd like that, but I'm just glad we can be together, that's all," she said, just as a knock came at the door.

Miriam looked at Timothy in surprise. They were not used to visitors at such a late hour, and the only people who ever called on them were the Jenkinsons. They would have long retired for the night. Timothy rose to answer, opening the door cautiously, as Miriam peered over his shoulder.

"Leah!" Miriam exclaimed, as her friend stepped inside without invitation, followed by Adam, the two of them looked angry and accusatory.

"So, we've found you," she said, as Adam advanced toward Timothy.

"You've got a lot of explaining to do," she said.

Miriam felt her heart hammering in her chest, she looked at Timothy to see his eyes wide a look of guilt on his face. Quickly, he moved to her side and took her hand.

# CHAPTER FIFTEEN

$\mathcal{M}$iriam was entirely taken aback by the sight of Leah and Adam. They had sent no word, and though she had written to tell them of the circumstances, she had not revealed the entire truth. As far as anyone was concerned, Miriam and Timothy were traveling around the state. No one knew anything of George or the events which had transpired in Philadelphia.

"It's not what you think it is..." Miriam said, stepping between Adam and Timothy.

"Are you sure about that?" Leah demanded.

Miriam nodded. "I know my own mind, Leah, it's..." she began, but just then, George began to cry, and now it was Leah's turn to look astonished, as Timothy hurried to see to him.

"A *boppli?*" she asked.

Miriam nodded. "We've all got some explaining to do," she replied. Over the next hours, she proceeded to tell Leah and Adam everything that had happened since she and Timothy had left Faith's Creek for Philadelphia.

Midway through her explanation, Timothy returned with George in his arms. Leah could hardly believe the sight of the *boppli* – explaining that Elizabeth was being looked after by her parents.

"We had to come and find you. There were rumors, you see, nothing definite, but... oh, I can't believe it," she said, shaking her head in amazement.

"I did the one thing I told you I wouldn't. But now I understand why you had to take Elizabeth. You had no choice. A *boppli* changes you, doesn't it?" Miriam said, and Leah nodded.

"You'd do anything for George, and I'd do anything for Elizabeth. Even if he's not your own, it makes no difference, there's a bond there," she said.

Miriam relaxed a little. Despite the surprise at their arrival, she was glad to see her friends and concluded her explanation by telling Leah and Adam that she and Timothy intended to remain in Pocono until nine months had passed. After that, they would return to Faith's Creek and pass George off as their own.

"And you really think this woman – Robyn – would let you?" Adam asked, a skeptical look in his eyes.

"She loves George, of course, she does. But she wants to be an actress and having a *boppli* – particularly one she didn't choose to have – can't be helpful to that. She knows he's better off with us, and we love him as though he was our own," Miriam replied, glancing at Timothy, who nodded.

Miriam believed this with all her heart, but what if she was wrong? Could she ever give her little boy back?

"ARE YOU CERTAIN ABOUT TIMOTHY?" Leah asked when later that night she and Miriam were alone.

Leah and Adam were to spend the night on the settee, and Miriam and Leah were washing up coffee cups in the kitchen, while the two men sat talking in the lounge.

"You know I wasn't before," Miriam replied, smiling.

Leah nodded and raised her eyebrows. "You did everything you could to avoid him. And now it's as though you can't get enough of him. Did you really mean to marry him?" she asked.

Miriam smiled. "Think about it this way. I had every intention of marrying Jonathan Kemp, but I found out some terrible things about him. It made me think again. But in the meantime, I found out a lot about Timothy, too, and I realized that just as I'd been wrong about Jonathan, I was wrong about Timothy, too," she said, knowing in her heart she had made the right decision. She loved Timothy and she loved George, she loved her family.

There was no doubting that marrying Timothy had been the right thing to do, and although it was not the wedding she had envisioned, it was still the love she had hoped for.

"I'm glad you're happy, Miriam. We were so worried about you. We thought the worst about him. Anyway, it all seems to have worked out here, though goodness knows what's going to happen when you get back to Faith's Creek," Leah replied, shaking her head.

"We'll cross that bridge when we come to it," Miriam replied.

She had been so busy settling into life in Pocono that the future still seemed a long way off. Nine months may as well have been a lifetime, but Miriam knew that eventually, she would have to confront her parents with the truth – at least the one she wanted them to know.

"It won't be easy," Leah said. "He won't look like a newborn."

"People won't ask... they might think bad things but they won't ask... will they?"

Leah thought for a moment. "Probably not. They won't want to know, but they will know. Why not tell the truth?"

"I prayed on it and I feel this is the way to go," Miriam said but was she sure?

"I understand."

"But you'll keep the secret, won't you?" Miriam asked.

Leah was still for a moment but then she nodded. "What are friends for?" she replied, smiling at Miriam, just as George began to cry.

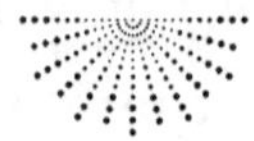

# CHAPTER SIXTEEN

It was nine months since the plan began, and Miriam, Timothy, and George had left Pocono behind and were on their way to Faith's Creek. It felt strange to leave behind the life they had built, and stranger, too, to be returning to what had once been so familiar. Miriam was nervous. She had told her parents nothing of the revelation that was about to come, only that she had news for them, and was looking forward to seeing them. It had been nearly a year since she had last set foot in Faith's Creek, and though she had Timothy at her side, she could not help but worry as to what the reaction in the community might be.

"Well, here we are," Timothy said, as the Greyhound bus came to the stop at the end of the lane closest to Faith's Creek.

He picked up their suitcases, and with George in a sling in Miriam's arms, the three of them stepped off the bus. The sweet scent of the harvest was blowing across the fields, and Miriam smiled, glad to be home, as she slipped her hand into Timothy's and the two of them walked together down the lane.

"I'll do the talking," she said, as they came to the gate of her parent's house, where the garden was as neat as ever. The porch door was open, and the scent of baking wafted through the air.

The sound of their footsteps brought her parents out from the kitchen, but the sight of George and Timothy soon caused the excited looks on their faces to fall. Wayne looked at them in astonishment, his face turning red with anger.

"Timothy Marshall, what is the meaning of this?" he demanded.

Timothy cleared his throat. "It's like this, sir..." he began, but Miriam interrupted him.

"We got married, and this is George, our son," she said, as Dawn stepped forward, shaking her head in disbelief.

"You got married and you didn't think to tell us? You had a son, and you didn't think to tell us?" she exclaimed.

Miriam nodded, a lump in her throat that threatened to choke her. "I'm sorry, it all happened so fast and..." she began.

Wayne's voice cut through the air like a whip. "Bopplis don't just happen, Miriam, they don't just fall out of the sky. You've taken advantage of my daughter." Red-faced he pointed at Timothy.

"No, *Daed*, he hasn't. We got married because we love one another," Miriam protested.

She had known her parents would not take kindly to the story and wondered once more if she should tell the truth. Only her daed had said he would not accept another boppli from someone else, her fears were proved. She did not want to argue, and she turned to her *mamm* with an imploring expression on her face.

"You can't expect us to believe that a *boppli* that size was born in wedlock," Dawn said.

Miriam's heart missed a beat. What now!

"I… it's not what you think. We fell in love, that's all, and we got married because of that. Timothy has a heart of gold. He wouldn't hurt anyone, and he'd never take advantage of me, not ever," she cried, the tears welling up in her eyes.

Timothy put his arm around her, and George woke up, his cries echoing over the garden.

"Can we come in, *Mamm?* George needs feeding," she said.

Dawn nodded. "All right, come in, all of you. We can't stand out here arguing about it," she said, ushering them inside.

Wayne shook his head.

"I know *Gott* has blessed us," Miriam said, holding her head up high as she stepped past her *daed*, who sighed and followed them inside.

Timothy stood awkwardly by the stove, as Dawn made coffee for them all, as Miriam took George out of his sling and placed him down on the rug.

"Oh, Miriam, he's beautiful. I just wish I'd known about him. I've got a grandson, but I didn't even know it," Dawn said, and she put down the coffee pot and came to look at George, who smiled up at her and gurgled.

"Why don't you come and see him, *Daed*? He'd be pleased to meet you," Miriam said, turning to her *daed*, who scowled.

"I'm sure you'll understand this is a lot to take in. I didn't give my permission for you to be married," he said.

Miriam sighed. "Then will you give it now?"

"Look at him, Wayne. He's just adorable," Dawn said, and reluctantly, her *daed* came to look down at the *boppli*, who was now blowing bubbles, as Dawn tickled his stomach.

"I want to know what your intentions are toward my daughter," Wayne asked, glancing up at Timothy.

Color rose on Timothy's cheeks. "I only want to be a good husband, sir," he replied.

"Call me Wayne, we are Amish, not Englischer," he snapped. "I suppose you'll want to stay," he said, turning to Miriam.

"That's why we came back," she replied.

It seemed her *daed's* demeanor was softening, though she could tell he was still angry. Her parents had always been strict, and Miriam knew they would be thinking about what might be said in the community when the facts were discovered.

"You can stay, this is your home," Dawn said, and she smiled at Timothy, whom she had known since childhood.

"I'm grateful, *denke*," Timothy said.

Miriam lifted George up into her arms and kissed him.

"Then we'd better get this one a bottle and to bed. There's still a lot to tell you about," she said, glancing at her parents, who exchanged looks with one another.

"A bottle!" Dawn said. "You don't feed him?"

There was a look in her mamm's eye, did she know?

"There is a lot to talk about," Wayne said, "I'm sure there is... will we get to hear it all?"

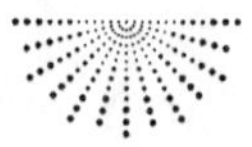

# CHAPTER SEVENTEEN

Several days passed, and Miriam found adapting to life back home in Faith's Creek a challenge. She had grown used to Timothy's company, the two of them getting by as best they could, and now she was home, her *mamm* and *daed* were a constant presence. While her *mamm* was pleased to have her home and had done much to make Timothy feel welcome, her *daed* remained suspicious of him. Miriam could only try her best to prove to him that she had made the right choice.

"Oh, I just put him down to sleep," Miriam said, as the sound of George crying came from the bedroom above.

"It's all right, I'll see to him," Timothy said, rising to his feet and hurrying up the stairs.

They had just sat down to dinner, and Dawn was serving out a casserole, the delightful smell of which had wafted through the house all afternoon.

"He certainly takes his duties seriously," Dawn said, glancing at Wayne, who grunted.

"He does," he replied.

"And he spent all afternoon digging over the vegetable patch at the back of the house for you," Miriam said.

Her *daed* looked at her in surprise.

"Did he?" he asked, and Miriam nodded.

It had been meant as a surprise, but Miriam was eager for her *daed to* realize what a good person Timothy could be. He had worked hard to prove himself, and she was proud of him for that. There was no doubting she had made the right match and, having caught a glimpse of Jonathan Kemp swaggering around the market the day before, Miriam knew she had avoided making a terrible mistake.

"And repaired the chicken coop. The foxes won't get in now," Dawn.

Wayne sighed and waved his hand as if driving them off. He was evidently torn between his prejudice and the facts.

"All right, all right, I get it," he said, as Timothy came quietly back down the stairs.

"He's sleeping, but for how long..." he said, taking his seat back at the table and glanced at Miriam with a smile.

"Timothy," Wayne said.

Startled, Timothy turned to him with an anxious expression. "Yes," he said, his voice sounding nervous.

"I know you've been trying hard to prove yourself. I'm sorry if I jumped to conclusions about you. When you have a daughter, you feel protective of her, and you don't like to think of her being taken advantage of," he said.

"I understand, and I would never..." he began, but Wayne interrupted him.

"Which is why I accept your actions as honorable. I can see how hard you've tried, and what a good *daed* you've been to George. You and Miriam have my blessing," he said.

Miriam's face broke into a smile. It was as if the heavens had opened and the light shone down on her.

"Oh, *Daed*, do you really mean it?" she asked.

For a moment he tugged on his beard. "I do, and I'm grateful to you, Timothy, for looking after Miriam when the man I thought she could trust turned out to be far from trustworthy," he replied.

Miriam had told her *daed* about Jonathan's antics in Philadelphia, though she had made no mention of Robyn or George's true parentage. To do so would be to cause a scandal, and Miriam had no intention of humiliating Jonathan in front of the community, as much as it may have served him right for her to do so. There had been no indication that he had guessed the truth about George, and Miriam was happy for that state of affairs to persist.

"Shall we take a walk?" Timothy asked when dinner was ended.

The two of them excused themselves, and with George asleep upstairs, and Dawn promising to keep an ear out for him stirring, they stepped out onto the porch and down the steps into the garden. Miriam slipped her arm into Timothy's, leaning her head on his shoulder as they walked together along the lane.

"I'm so glad my *daed* had a change of heart," she said.

"Me, too. I've really tried so hard, but I didn't know how he felt," Timothy said.

"He's made it clear, now. You're one of the family, and that's all that matters. I'm so glad we did this – all of it," she said, and Timothy nodded.

"Me too. I wouldn't have had it any other way," he said, and they paused on the lane and turned to one another.

Miriam smiled up at him, astonished at the change which had come over her since last they had stood there all those months ago. Back then, the very thought of having anything to do with Timothy Marshall had filled her with dread, but now she could not imagine life without him. She loved him, and with George, their family was complete.

"I really do love you, Timothy," she whispered, leaning up to kiss him. Now that his beard had grown she delighted in the feel of it as they kissed.

He held her in his arms, and she knew that in that moment she had everything she had ever desired.

"And I love you, too, Miriam, and I'll do anything to keep you and George safe, I promise," he said, and in those words, Miriam knew there was the truth, and nothing but the truth. A truth she could hold onto and believe in for the rest of her life, thankful to *Gott* for leading her in the right direction and bringing her to happiness at last.

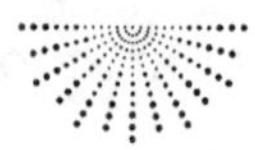

# CHAPTER EIGHTEEN

"There now, don't you look a picture?" Miriam said, as she kissed George on the forehead and lifted him up to put him in his stroller.

With, Timothy, George, and her parents, she had been invited to a potluck at the Hochstetlers. Nervous, Miriam had been busy for the past hour getting ready. George was dressed in a blue knitted jumper made by Dawn. Miriam was looking forward to seeing him with Samuel and Elizabeth, the three adopted babies of the three best friends.

"We'd better hurry, we'll be late," Timothy said, and they set off as a family, walking along the lane toward the Hochstetler house. As they got closer, the smell of barbecuing meat wafted over the garden.

"I'm so glad you're here," Leah exclaimed, coming to greet them at the gate. With a gleeful smile, she embraced Miriam, ushering them into the garden, where further greetings were exchanged.

It seemed that most of the community had turned out for the potluck, and Miriam could see Alma and Sawyer, amongst the crowd, along with Bishop Beiler and Sarah, who waved to them. Feeling a little overwhelmed, Miriam pushed George's stroller across the grass, followed by Timothy and her parents.

"You're looking so well, Miriam," Sarah said, kissing her on the cheek.

Miriam smiled. She had confided everything to Sarah, and apart from Timothy, she was the only one who knew the truth.

"*Denke.* I'm so glad to be back in Faith's Creek," Miriam said.

Sarah smiled a warm and welcoming smile, one that didn't judge.

"Congratulations to you both, though I'm just sorry I didn't get the chance to marry you, so to speak," Bishop Amos Beiler said, laughing at his own joke.

"Oh, I know, we wanted that, too, but we wanted to be married and..." Miriam began...

Amos shook his head. "You don't need to explain. The important thing is that the two of you are married and *Gott* has blessed your union. That much is obvious," he said, looking down at George and smiling.

"I feel very blessed," Miriam told him, glancing at Timothy with a smile.

Just then, Alma came hurrying over with Samuel, whom she set down on the grass next to where the others were standing.

"Let's see them all together," she said, glancing at Leah, who nodded.

"I'll get Elizabeth," she said.

Miriam set George down next to Samuel, the two babies looking at one another curiously.

"They're so cute together," Alma said, and she and Miriam kneeled down next to the *kinner*. In that moment, Miriam could not have felt prouder to be a *mamm* to George.

Bishop Beiler and Sarah excused themselves, and Timothy was called by Adam to help with the barbecue, leaving the two women alone. A few moments later, Leah returned with Elizabeth, and the three *bopplis* were placed next to each other, all looking slightly confused at their encounter.

"Don't they look adorable, we're so lucky to have them," Leah said, and Miriam and Alma agreed.

"They've all been through so much, even if they don't realize it," Miriam said, and Leah slipped her hand into Miriam's and squeezed it.

"We know George isn't yours, Miriam..." she said.

Miriam looked at her in astonishment. "But he is..." she began...

Leah shook her head. "Adam met Robyn. She told him what happened. But it doesn't matter. You're George's *mamm*, just like I'm Samuel's *mamm* and Leah's Elizabeth's *mamm*. We love these *kinner*, and we'd die for them – that's true love, and nothing can take that away from us," she said.

A voice behind her interrupted them. "And what about their *daeds*?"

Miriam turned in horror to find Jonathan Kemp staring at her angrily.

She had tried to put him out of her mind and had avoided having anything to do with him. He knew she and Timothy were married, but as far as he was concerned, she believed he knew nothing of George's true parentage. Now she faced him defiantly, stepping protectively between him and George, as Leah and Alma did the same.

"And what's that supposed to mean?" Alma demanded.

"I know all about this. I know that's Robyn's baby. Which means he's my son," Jonathan replied, pointing at George, who was happily playing with Samuel and Elizabeth, oblivious to the row developing above him.

"And you think you're fit to be a *daed*?" Leah asked.

Jonathan seemed somewhat taken aback by these words, and his face turned red with anger.

"You would question that? What right have you..." he began, but Leah interrupted him.

"And what right have you to make claims like that? You left that poor woman high and dry, just like you left half a dozen other women," she said.

Alma nodded. "It takes more than biology to be a parent, Jonathan. Where were you when Robyn gave birth? Where were you when your son needed holding and comforting? Where were you for any of it? A parent is made in love, not by rights."

"I love George as my own, and Timothy loves him, too. He's the very best of *daeds*, more so than you could ever be." Miriam felt her anger welling up against Jonathan, who seemed surprised by the force of her response.

Miriam disliked conflict, she had not confronted Jonathan over his infidelity, but now she could barely hold back, angry not only for herself but for all the women whom Jonathan had so ill-treated.

"I could tell everyone what you've done," he retorted, but the three women only shook their heads, facing him as one.

"We know all about you, Adam found all the women you hurt. You have a string of *kinner* across the state – and that's a pretty big welfare bill, isn't it?" Leah said as Jonathan faltered.

"I... you don't know that," he said.

Leah smiled and laughed. "Well, there's Robyn, Cheryl, Deborah, Elizabeth... do you want me to go on. *Boppli* George here, has three half brothers, Michael, Dickson..." she began.

Jonathan raised his hands for her to stop. "All right, all right, enough, already," he cried, just as Timothy, Adam, and Sawyer came up.

"Is everything all right?" Timothy asked, lifting George up in his arms.

Miriam nodded, putting her arm around him and kissing George on the forehead. "It's fine. Jonathan was just congratulating us on having a healthy, happy *boppli* in our lives," she said, and Timothy smiled.

"That's very kind of you," he said, and he held out his hand to Jonathan, who reluctantly took it.

"Congratulations to you all," he said, and with that, he turned on his heels and slunk off into the crowd.

"I think that's the last we'll see of him," Alma said, picking up Samuel, as Leah did the same with Elizabeth.

As Jonathan wandered away, Miriam felt her eyes pulled to the left. There she saw Bishop Beiler looking at Jonathan and he did not look happy. She whispered a prayer of thanks, she knew the bishop would take care of this. Jonathan would change his ways or he would have to leave.

"Is this the first time we've all been together?" Leah asked, and the others nodded.

"Three little families, all of them a little different, but nonetheless special for it," Miriam said, looking around at her friends and feeling a sudden and overwhelming sense of blessing.

"It's not about biology," Alma said, "it's about love."

"And these children are loved," Leah said, as the three babies sat in their *mamm's* arms, all of them with smiles on their faces.

"Well, I think it's time we introduced them to a good old-fashioned potluck," Sawyer said, as the call came for the food to be blessed, and Bishop Beiler climbed onto an upturned crate to make the prayer.

"And a toast to the future," Miriam said, glancing up at Timothy, who smiled.

"A happy future for us all," he said, and everyone agreed.

# EPILOGUE

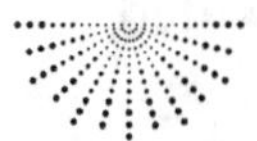

It was a year later, and the height of summer in Faith's Creek. Miriam and Timothy had joined Leah, Alma, Adam, and Sawyer for a picnic by the creek, and of course, the three *kinner* had come, too, joined by a new addition.

"Not too close to the water's edge," Alma called out, as Samuel ran across the grass.

She was sitting on the picnic rug cradling her newborn son Caleb in her arms, and Leah was sitting opposite her, heavily pregnant, leaning on Adam, all of them enjoying the sunshine. Sawyer had gone to fetch more drinks, and Timothy and Miriam were handing around the boxes of food they had brought with them, the heat of the day making all of them lethargic – save for the three *kinner*, who had grown boisterous with the passing months and were now playing on the grass nearby.

"Isn't this lovely," Miriam said, helping herself to a sausage roll and coming to sit next to Alma so that she could look at Caleb, who was fast asleep in his *mamm's* arms.

"If only it could be summer every day. I always think these long hot summers will never end," Alma replied.

"No more rumspringa, no more Philadelphia, we're all grown up," Leah said, sitting up and stretching out with a yawn.

"I like that," Miriam said, glancing at Timothy with a smile.

It had been quite a year for them all. Miriam and Timothy had adopted George as their own, with Robyn's blessing, and now rented a house and smallholding about a mile from the home of her parents. Alma had given birth to Caleb, and Leah had announced the happy news of her pregnancy. She was right, they were all growing up, and Miriam was thankful that at last, she had discovered the happiness she deserved.

"Not long for you now, Leah," Miriam said, passing her friend a piece of seed cake, just as Sawyer returned with a crate of lemonade.

"It can't come soon enough. My ankles are swollen, I've had terrible morning sickness, and I can hardly sleep," she said, sighing and shaking her head.

"It'll all be worth it. When you hold that *boppli* in your arms, you'll forget everything you went through. It's strange – I was just the same. But now I'd do it all again, really, I would," Alma said, looking down at Caleb, who was still asleep in her arms.

He had been born only a month before, and the other *kinner* had been fascinated at the sight of another *boppli* in their midst.

"They play so well together, don't they?" Miriam said, watching, as Samuel, Elizabeth, and George passed a ball to one another.

"They'll be friends for life, just like we are," Alma replied, and Miriam nodded, smiling at them both, and grateful to *Gott* for the friendship they shared.

"We've certainly made some memories together. But it's all worked out well in the end," Leah replied, as Sawyer handed round the bottles of lemonade.

"I got them cold from the store, but it's so hot today they're already warm," he said, opening a bottle and taking a long draught.

"It's still refreshing. We'll dream of today when the snow comes," Alma said, and both Miriam and Leah groaned.

"Oh, don't say that, Alma. I get so depressed in the winter," Leah said, but Alma only laughed.

"You won't have time to get depressed, you'll be too busy with your new arrival," she said, and Miriam glanced at Timothy, who nodded.

She had some news to share with her friends but had wanted to wait until the right moment to do so. Now, she cleared her throat, glancing at George and the other *kinner*, who were still playing happily on the grass.

"There's something we want to tell you all," she said, slipping her hand into Timothy's. The others looked at her curiously, though the news would surely come as no surprise.

"Are you…" Leah said, a smile coming over her face, and Miriam nodded.

"I'm going to have a *boppli*. It's still some months off – you'll beat me to it, Leah, don't worry. But Doctor Yoder confirmed it on Friday. I can't wait," she said, and the others now offered their congratulations.

"Oh, Miriam, I'm so pleased for you, that's wonderful news," Alma exclaimed.

"We felt the time was right. I know we've had a lot to deal with – the adoption, and moving house, but… well, it seemed right. All of it seemed right," Miriam replied.

"It's *Gott's* will for you," Leah said, and Miriam could only agree.

Throughout all of this, Miriam had felt *Gott's* presence with her, gently guiding and encouraging her. She had prayed often, and though at times she had wondered if her prayers were heard, she knew now that *Gott* had led her to the right place. This was what was meant to be, and with the arrival of their second child, their family would be complete.

"Well, I think this deserves a toast," Sawyer said, raising his bottle of lemonade.

"To families, and the future," Adam said, and all of them toasted that happy occasion, each with much to look forward to.

LATER THAT AFTERNOON, after they had finished their picnic, Miriam, Timothy, and George were walking together by the creek. George was fast asleep in his sling, and Miriam had her arm through Timothy's, the two of them walking side by side, as she rested her head on his shoulder.

"It's been a lovely day. I'm so pleased we told them all about the *boppli*. I can't wait," she said.

"We've certainly had some changes this past year. My life's totally different," Timothy replied.

He had no family in Faith's Creek and marrying Miriam had given him the family he had always longed for. Miriam knew how happy he was – he told her that every day, and he could not wait to be *daed* once again.

"Mine is, too. But all for the better," she replied.

"I never imagined being where we are now. I never imagined being married to you and having a *boppli* together.

Well, I imagined it. But I didn't think it would happen," Timothy said, pausing, and turning to her, with a look of love on his face, as he put his hand gently on the back of George's head.

"I didn't either, and I feel terrible for not seeing that before. I was so caught up with my feelings for that man... I couldn't see the good thing in front of me," Miriam replied, and she leaned up and kissed Timothy on the lips, smiling at him and putting her arms around him, so that George was cradled between them.

"Thank you for loving me," he said, but she shook her head.

"It's me who should thank you," she replied.

There was much which had been unexpected, but Miriam had come to trust in *Gott's* plan for her, knowing she was led along the right paths. Timothy, George, her friends – everything had happened for a reason, and now she looked to the future with happiness, knowing she had everything she needed.

"I haven't done anything. It's this little one we should thank – he brought us together," Timothy said, gazing down at the sleeping George, who stirred as Miriam kissed him gently on the forehead.

"He's just perfect, and so will our next one be, too. A boy or a girl, it doesn't matter, they'll be loved, just as George is. We've all been blessed. It was meant to be, it was the miracle we longed for," Miriam said, slipping her hand into Timothy's as they walked on by the creek.

Life had not turned out as she expected – nor had it done for any of her friends. *Gott* had a way of surprises, and though Miriam would never have guessed the course her life would take, she could not have been happier than in that moment. Leah had been right, it was love that made a family, and it was in love that Miriam looked to the future knowing that whatever it held, she was blessed.

Did you miss:

Love and Faith

SARAH MILLER

# Or Elizabeth A Baby Blessing

Anna Sutter had a good life, all things considered. *Gott* had graced her with a loving *mamm* and *daed,* and a younger *schweschder* who seemed to shine as brightly as the sun.

When there were so many people in the world who had not even one person to care for them, she knew that she was blessed beyond measure. That was what made her pervasive sadness all the more difficult to bear.

She lived in an Amish community called Faith's Creek, along with the rest of her *familye.* It was the place she had been born, as had her parents before her. She had *nee* doubt at all that it would be where she lived still when it was finally time for her to go to be with *Gott.*

She thought it was probably one of the loveliest places in all of the world, although she had nothing to compare it to, and she was happy enough to stay there for the whole of her life. It wasn't where she was that made her unhappy, it was who she was inside, and she thought that must be a good deal worse.

She was a slight young woman, slender trending on the side of frail. Her deep chestnut hair was always up under the covering of her *kapp*. She was careful never to let a single strand stray out of place if she could help it. She did not like the idea of giving people a reason for her to be seen.

Her eyes were wide and almost as dark as her hair, and her skin was as pale as a fresh container of cream. Against the dark hues of the blue dresses that were her daily uniform, she worried that the extremity of her fairness made her stand out like a white sheet fluttering across a night-darkened sky. The thought alone made her tremble with dread, and it made her more than a little weary to venture outdoors more than was strictly necessary.

Perhaps worst of the long list of things she believed weren't quite right about her, was the fact that at twenty-years-old, she remained unwed. Not only was she still unmarried, when many of her peers had already begun their own happy *familye's,* but she also had nary a prospect or hope of being courted anytime soon. It seemed to her that, aside from her always loving parents and *schweschder,* nobody in Faith's Creek wanted her or would really care if she were suddenly gone.

"Such a foolish way to think," she chastised herself as she tugged mercilessly at her needle and thread. "Such a waste of energy. What does it matter if you're wanted by others at all? You contribute. You work as hard as you can to help make this *haus* a home."

She nodded to herself, glancing down at the ever-growing pile of completed mending beside her for reassuring proof. It was true that she was a hard worker, and one who never complained, and she knew her parents appreciated that about her.

Unfortunately, it was also true that if she were never able to find a man who wanted to take her for his *fraa,* she would undoubtedly prove to be a burden as her parents moved into their golden years of age. They would have to continue to care for her long past the point when parents were meant to be relieved of that task. The mere thought of it was enough to make her shudder, and her eyes well up with tears.

"*Ach*, here you are!" Anna's *schweschder*, Ruth, exclaimed from the open screen door of the back porch. "I've been looking for you all over. I thought you had gone and disappeared."

"*Nee*, I've been right here the whole time," Anna protested, her heart hammering in her chest as she tried in vain to recover from her start. "And you frightened me half to death. You shouldn't sneak up on people like that, Ruth. You really shouldn't."

"I know," Ruth said with a dramatic sigh that wasn't quite able to make up for the glint of mischief shining in her cornflower eyes. "But sometimes, I just can't seem to help myself. And, anyway, I really was looking for you, and for what felt like the longest time. Have you been out here all day?"

"Why, I don't know," Anna answered with a small frown of confusion.

She looked out from beneath the porch's comfortably weathered ceiling and gazed up at the sky, trying to determine what time it was. Truth be told, she didn't have the first clue how long she had been out there on her own. That was one of the hazards of being a person who spent most of her waking hours on her own. Time had a way of losing itself, and sometimes, of disappearing altogether.

"Well, I think you have been," Ruth said decisively, her hands on her hips as she surveyed Anna's day's work with a scrutinizing eye. "And I think it's enough for today. It's time to put your work away, too."

"*Ach,* really?" Anna asked, laughing despite herself. "And what brought you to that conclusion?"

"My keen powers of observation," Ruth said, her expression kept serious for only a moment before she collapsed into a fit of giggles that Anna couldn't help but join in.

And that was the thing about Ruth, the thing that everybody who met her couldn't help but notice. Ruth was the sort of girl that people just wanted to be around, even if they couldn't quite put their finger on why. She was funny and kind, silly, and a little bit wild, and all of those things were absolutely contagious.

In short, Anna believed that her sweet, sixteen-year-old *schweschder* was all of the things that she herself was not. Whereas Anna was likely to blend seamlessly into the background of any gathering she was forced to attend, Ruth was always like a bright, shining star in a crowd.

Everyone wanted to be around her, and although she was still just a little bit too young to begin a courtship, it was already widely understood who she would eventually marry. It was understood with a confidence that Anna couldn't remember ever having about anything in her life.

Ruth and a boy named Jonathan Kemp had been thick as thieves for as long as anyone could remember, and their friendship seemed to be naturally evolving into something far deeper. While Jonathan was about to leave for his *Rumspringa,* people expected that when he returned to Faith's Creek, he and Ruth would begin courting. They would be wed, and Anna would officially be surpassed by her lovely younger *schweschder.*

"I'm serious, Anna," she whined now, reaching for Anna's hand and trying to tug her onto her feet. "It's time to put this away. Don't you want to have a little bit of adventure in your life?"

"What?" Anna asked with surprise and not a little bit of dread. "*Nee,* of course not. What are you going on about, anyhow?"

"Nothing," Ruth answered, a pretty pout on her pert, sixteen-year-old lips. "I'm just saying that it might not be such a bad thing for you to do something other than work and shut yourself away in the *haus*."

"It's a *wunderbaar haus*," Anna snapped back, her tone more severe than she intended, although she didn't seem to make it otherwise. "And I don't mind the work. I'm happy to do it. I'm happy to be useful to our parents. I think they need me to do what I do, anyhow. What would they think if I just ran off?"

"They would be pleased for you to have a little time to yourself," Ruth answered immediately, and with a confidence that Anna didn't think she had ever felt before in her life. "I was talking to *Mamm*..."

"About me?" Anna interrupted, finally getting to her feet as Ruth had wanted her to all along. "The two of you were talking about me without me being there?"

"*Jah*, but not anything bad," Ruth insisted, finally showing the faintest hint of uncertainty. "I was telling her that I wished the two of us spent more time together. Time outside of the *haus*, and she said she thought that was a lovely idea. She is the one who bade me come and find you. She told me you should come with me to game night."

That stopped Anna cold. The idea that two of the people she loved most in the world had come together to speak about the extent to which she was isolating herself made her feel exposed and ashamed. It was the very feeling she feared most, and so she kept herself apart as if it might keep her safe.

And yet, at the same time, there was a part of her that saw what Ruth was saying now as an opportunity. She saw it as a chance being offered to her, one that she was sorely tempted to take. Perhaps she wasn't destined to live out her days alone, after all, as unlikely as the possibility seemed. Maybe forcing herself to come out of her shell a little would offer her one of *Gott's* many blessings and rewards.

"*Jah,*" she said softly before she had time to convince herself not to speak at all.

"What?" Ruth asked, her eyes growing wide with disbelief. "What did you say?"

"I said *Jah,*" Anna repeated, smiling at her *schweschder's* obvious delight despite the butterflies fluttering wildly in her stomach. "All right. I'll accompany you into town tonight, just so long as you promise not to try and turn it into a habit."

Instead of answering, Ruth threw her arms around Anna's neck. Anna understood that Ruth's failure to agree to her terms meant that there would likely be similar requests in the future. At the moment, however, she found that she didn't really care. She was going to allow herself an adventure, and despite it being a small one, she was excited for what may come to pass.

Grab Amish Love in Faith's Creek a super value 15 Book Box Set now for FREE with Kindle Unlimited.

**All my books are FREE on Kindle Unlimited**

If you love Amish Romance, the sweet, clean stories of Sarah Miller you can join me for the latest news on upcoming books http://eepurl.com/bdEdSn

**These are some of my reader favorites:**

Amish Spring Baby

A Love Tested

Find all Sarah's books on Amazon and click the yellow follow button

+ Follow

This book is dedicated to the wonderful Amish people and the faithful life that they live.

Go in peace, my friends.

As an independent author, Sarah relies on your support. If you enjoyed this book, please leave a review on Amazon or Goodreads.

# ABOUT THE AUTHOR

Sarah Miller was born in Pennsylvania and spent her childhood close to the Amish people. Weekends were spent doing chores; quilting or eventually babysitting in the community. She grew up to love their culture and the simple lifestyle and had many Amish friends. The one thing that you can guarantee when you are near the Amish, Sarah believes is that you will feel close to God.

Many years later she married Martin who is the love of her life and moved to England. There she started to write stories about the Amish. Recently after a lot of persuasion from her best friend she has decided to publish her stories. They draw on inspiration from her relationship with the Amish and with God and she hopes you enjoy reading them as much as she did writing them. Many of the stories are based on true events but names have been changed and even though they are authentic at times artistic license has been used.

Sarah likes her stories simple and to hold a message and they help bring her closer to her faith. She currently lives in Yorkshire, England with her husband Martin and seven very spoiled chickens.

She would love to meet you on Facebook at https://www.facebook.com/SarahMillerBooks

Sarah hopes her stories will both entertain and inspire and she wishes that you go with God.